Ana Isabel

a respectable girl

Antonia Palacios

Ana Isabel: A Respectable Girl

Translated by RoseAnna Mueller

Universitas Press
Montreal

Universitas Press
Montreal

www.universitaspress.com

Modern Classics Series Editor: Cristina Artenie

First published in June 2016

Library and Archives Canada Cataloguing in Publication

Palacios, Antonia
[Ana Isabel, una niña decente. English]
        Ana Isabel : a respectable girl / Antonia Palacios ; translated
by RoseAnna Mueller.

Translation of: Ana Isabel, una niña decente.
ISBN 978-0-9950291-1-8 (paperback)

        I. Mueller, RoseAnna M., translator II. Title. III. Title: Ana
Isabel, una niña decente. English

PQ8550.26.A48A6313 2016   863.64   C2016-903596-4

TABLE OF CONTENTS

Acknowledgments vii

Translator's Note ix

Introduction: Pride and Poverty xiii

Antonia Palacios: A Chronology xix

Ana Isabel: A Respectable Girl

Candelaria Town Square 5

Two Funerals 9

Carnival Sunday 15

The Map of Venezuela 22

The Kiskadee 27

Confession 31

The Silver Tray 38

A Voice Sings from Afar 46

The Field Trip 51

The Deer 58

Who Killed Butterfly? 65

The Piñata 75

Delirium 84

Little Black Eusebio Died 90

The Lizard 97

Ana Isabel Behind the Bars 102

Glossary 111

Afterword: A Few Word from a Reader 113

Acknowledgments

I am grateful to Mariantonia Frías Melchert, the author's granddaughter, who contacted her father, Carlos Eduardo Frías, and who gave me permission to translate and publish the English translation of *Ana Isabel, una niña decente*. My thanks to Gregory Zambrano for putting me in touch with Ms. Frías Melchert.

I would like to thank Michele Lee, Executive Director of Centro Venezolano Americano, who read the first draft of the translation and who suggested I work with Miguel Frontado to help with Venezuelan regionalisms. Miguel, who had never read the book, was deeply moved by it. Thank you both for your interest and your help with this project.

Maria Gracia Pardo, University of Miami, carefully read through the second draft and made valuable suggestions. I thank Maria Gracia for her painstaking work and for her encouragement in helping little Ana Isabel find a home for an English-reading public. Clara Herrera, Lake Forest College, found many similarities with Ana Isabel's Venezuelan childhood and her own childhood memories in Colombia, and I thank her for her close reading, her suggestions and her encouragement.

For their friendship, and for their ongoing support I wish to thank Carolyn Hulse, Kathleen Reinmuth, and Sandy Sporleder, who read my translation and shared in Ana Isabel's life story.

My everlasting gratitude to Bob, for sharing whatever comes next.

Translator's Note

Antonia Palacios focused on introducing a new way of expressing female subjectivity. Her novel has many regionalisms (*venezolanismos*) that form a part of the written and spoken aspects of Spanish in Venezuela. I consulted several native speakers to help me with the translation.

Palacios wrote *Ana Isabel, una niña decente* to reflect her memories of growing up in a square or plaza in Caracas in the 1920s. The child's language is mediated through the memories of an adult. As the narrator matures, so does the nature of her language. Ana Isabel becomes aware of the racial and economic inequalities in her life. Her descriptions become more poetical and sophisticated.

One of the first challenges in translating the novel was how to interpret the many childhood games that are described. This was a time when children played outdoors and spent hours together unsupervised playing games that are now forgotten. Many of the games are no longer played, but they were an important part of childhood life when Caracas was a small collection of neighborhoods whose focus was its town square. Some of the games have current equivalents, such as Cops and Robbers or Bogey Man.

Another choice was determining when to translate the names of plants, trees and flowers that would have no equivalent to an English-speaking reader. Other issues were translating articles of attire, such as "alpargatas" which could be translated as "sandals" or "espadrilles," but whose Spanish word suggests class and social status. Like the Mexican "huarache" it is a very specific kind of footwear, a rope-soled inexpensive sandal. "Arepas" are the staple dish in Venezuela and I kept the word and added its translation in the glossary. Keeping words such as "alpargata," "arepa," and the names of local flora and fauna in the original text provides more authenticity.

Antonia Palacios was a poet. She did not leave her poetic voice behind when she began to write her novel. In some cases, since a child is the narrator, many of the passages are straightforward and can be translated literally. At other times, the prose becomes lyrical. I retained her unconventional and idiosyncratic use of punctuation. Palacios uses few commas, no hyphens, and often ends her sentences with ellipses, or she places an exclamation mark before the ellipses, as in "!..."

The Monte Ávila Editores edition (1969) includes a "Vocabulario" or Glossary for the many plants, animals, foods and colloquial expressions used in the novel. One example of a bird mentioned in the novel occurs in Chapter 5, "El Cristofué." This chapter begins with the description of a kiskadee. The Spanish name is a play on words, since Cristofué sounds like "Christ was" in Spanish, which presents a problem when translating this play on words into English. Another challenge was how to translate the speech of the black servants. They often do not use full sentences or they drop the endings of words. Several readers suggested using something like Black English, or English as it was spoken in the rural South to represent the servants' speech. Staying true to these speech patterns acknowledges the complexities of the time in which Palacios lived.

The chants and words that accompany the games and the rhythms and meanings of nursery rhymes must also be compensated for. "Poco a poco mister Payer" is the expression the children used to convey the sound the train makes. In Spanish, it imitates the rhythm of the train running down the tracks, and it can't be conveyed into English literally, so I translated it as the "clickety-clack" rhyme we use in the U.S.

Ultimately, I want the reader to be able to experience young Ana Isabel's world though her insights, her imagery and her creative use of language as the reader enters her private world with all its joys, sorrows, and longings. I hope that my translation of this important writer's work that has not been translated into English will prove valuable to a non-Spanish reading public.

I lived in Venezuela as a Fulbright Scholar from 2002 to 2003, teaching Latin American Women's Literature in Spanish at the Universidad de los Andes in Mérida. It was there that I first read Antonia Palacios's remarkable novel, and for that I am grateful.

RoseAnna Mueller

*To the memory of Antonia Palacios
and to all young Ana Isabels.*

RoseAnna Mueller

Pride and Poverty: The World of Ana Isabel

Ana Isabel, una niña decente was dedicated to Antonia Palacios' children, Mariantonia and Fernán and to her husband Carlos Eduardo. In the introduction to Palacios' *Obras Completas* (*Complete Works*, 1980), Fernán Frias wonders about the work's intended audience. Was his mother's novel meant to be read by young readers, or did she intend it to be read by adults? He concludes that both the young and the old can enjoy the novel. He points to an "innocent sensuality" in the novel and describes the structure of the novel as a collage, a series of paintings in which the narrative and the descriptive combine, so that a narrative thread unifies the episodes. He concludes that Ana Isabel develops as a person, not just as a character (xii).

The novel takes place in the Caracas of 1920s and offers a vision of life at the very beginning of the century before urban development when the country still possessed a rural soul while Europe was recovering after World War I. Caracas expanded in 1925 and due to the discovery of petroleum, many rural dwellers emigrated to the city. The novel describes life within the walls and patios of a house before the advent of tall buildings. These were colonial houses with interior patios, with red tile roofs and overhanging eaves. They were closed-off fortresses, protecting and sheltering the family. Women worked in their homes, employed in cottage industries making sweets, sewing, selling milk, taking in laundry, or, as in Ana Isabel's mother's case, making cigarette boxes. Ana Isabel grows up in her little universe with her mother, father, brother and black servants in a proper and proud household where, despite the lack of money, and in some cases the bare necessities, life goes staunchly on. Ana Isabel is unsure about her family's economic circumstances; compared to the poor who live in the slums, she is not as poverty-stricken as they are. Compared to the rich schoolmates with government connections and her wealthy relatives, she is poor. Ana Isabel's mother, identified only as Mrs. Alcántara, looks down on outsiders and tries to pass on her suspicions concerning race and class to her daughter. Ana Isabel questions these assumptions and wants to right the social inequality she sees all around her. In her novel, Palacios combines her perspective as a poet with the ability to interpret the experiences of a young girl. She evokes the sensibility and innocence of a child using free, indirect speech as she describes her inner thoughts and tries to make sense of the world around her.

Another insight the novel offers is into the public world of the plaza or the town square, where the children all play freely and Ana Isabel makes friends. When the novel was written, there was no television and children played many games outdoors. Many of them are forgotten games that used to be played in the still-rural plazas of Venezuela when Caracas was a collection of small neighborhoods or parishes, each with its town square and church. Children of all social classes mixed and mingled in the plaza that was the focus of their community. Ana Isabel is free to join in these games and befriend the other children while she is in the plaza, but she would not be allowed to bring them into her home, and there are homes she would not be welcome to. Some of the games are "rondas" in which children form a circle and hold hands and sing songs. Others are more like our own hide-and-seek or cops and robbers. Ana Isabel attends school along with the daughters of rich and powerful families, which further exposes her to racial and social inequalities. She questions the strict gender roles and awakens to the reality of the dictatorial legacy of Juan Vicente Gómez with its corruption and political favors. Gómez was the de-facto ruler of Venezuela from 1908 to 1935, a time of upheaval and repression, and it is this society that Ana Isabel grows up in. The novel examines the complexities and contradictions of growing up in such a society, especially for women.

Although she lives in a patriarchal society, fathers are conspicuously absent in the novel. Ana Isabel's father is ill and unemployed. Her friend Pepe's father appears one day to offer a coin to his mother and prides himself that one day his son will be "macho" like himself. Otilia's father simply disappears one day. Fathers leave, and mothers and children are left to fend for themselves. Ana Isabel wonders why her poor friends do not have fathers. Since this is a taboo subject, she relies on her black nanny and the black domestic to answer these questions for her. The patriarchal legacy of the Roman Catholic Church also comes into play as Ana Isabel prepares to make her first confession before she can receive her First Holy Communion. She learns about sin from both her teacher and the priest, as she struggles with her sexual innocence and sensual nature.

Antonia Palacios created a literature that recalls its national past while placing it in a new modernist context. Like her predecessor, Teresa de la Parra (1889-1936), Palacios took into account Venezuela's colonial heritage. Palacios was first and foremost a poet. With its first printing in 1949, the sixteen chapters of her novel sparked great interest. It was a literary event that, given its literary antecedents, displayed the narrative capacity of a writer who was primarily known for her collections of poetry. But the novel takes on a confessional and autobiographical tone as Palacios experimented with new ways of representing a young girl's reality. Many comparisons can be made between Antonia Palacios and Teresa de la Parra's groundbreaking works. Palacios follows in her footsteps and borrows both from *Mama Blanca's Memoirs* and *Iphigenia, the diary of a young girl who wrote because she was bored,* to the point of using some of the same names for the characters. Both novels have a pious maiden Aunt Clara and a wise black servant named Gregoria. Teresa de la Parra sometimes wrote under the pen name Fru-Fru, which is the name of Ana Isabel's doll. Both novels leave the reader wondering what will happen to these two young women living in Caracas and what will change in their personal worlds while Caracas undergoes its own changes. Both *Ana Isabel* and *Mama Blanca's Memoirs* are semi-autobiographical depictions of a young girl growing up in a changing Venezuela. Some things that hold fast are the old Creole families' attitudes toward race and class, entrenched in old colonial values they are reluctant to give up. Having connections to the new booming petroleum industry and the reigning regime are eroding status once based on race and ancestry. Both novels show the restrictions placed on women in a patriarchal society; they have limited choices and limited options. They examine the preoccupation with family pride, respectability, exclusivity, and the desire to carry on traditions brought over by the Spanish conquistadors. Creoles were members of a social class who were typically the land-holding descendants of the first families of Venezuela, entitled to bear coats-of-arms as witness to their illustrious genealogies. This class clings fast to its pride; and proof of their Spanish lineage was important to them. Both novels can be considered failed *Bildungsromans*: the heroine of *Iphigenia*, Maria Eugenia, succumbs to the societal mandates placed on her and marries for money. Will Ana Isabel be forced to follow in her footsteps? Both authors employed an autobiographical approach that allowed them to question modernization and the social, economic and historical changes that were taking place in Venezuela.

Ana Isabel represents a step forward in the expression of a feminine element in Venezuelan literature and it is written in a style that breaks with the symbolic realist genre so much in vogue at the time. While Palacios continued in the style of her predecessor, she differs from her by inaugurating a new form of expression with poetic overtones. This novel's language is spontaneous and lyrical. Its simple, spare yet lush language communicates the emotions and inner thoughts of its young protagonist forcefully. Its visual images make the novel an outstanding case of clarity of expression, a rare case in the Venezuelan literature being written at the time. The novel is one of expressive economy, and is free of high-sounding rhetorical formulas. It succeeds in transmitting the evolution of a young girl as she heads toward adolescence. A child's world comes into conflict with the adult world; her active imagination comes into conflict with reality. Every observation triggers deeply felt emotions as Ana Isabel awakens to the social and economic inequality of her world, the world of the Candelaria Square tucked away in a corner of Caracas. She becomes aware of the political situation that confers status and privilege, the realities of the adult world, and she witnesses several deaths.

Her black friend Eusebio dies. The death of children seems to be commonplace. Ana Isabel witnesses a very elaborate funeral given for the Minister's daughter that stops traffic. These are contrasted with the funerals given for a poor child who will be buried in a plain wood box and the funeral of the humble shoemaker whose neighbors pitch in to help bury him.

The new political order in Venezuela of the 1920s brought about a new economy and its own code of social stratification which is in conflict with Ana Isabel's parents' definition of what is proper, noble and "respectable." The new order is being redefined by the dictatorship and the discovery of oil. But the old political order is difficult to shake off and it too contains its own set of rigid, and at times opaque, conventions which Ana Isabel wonders about and questions. As Ana Isabel approaches her adolescence and young womanhood, she struggles to adjust her notions and beliefs acquired in her childhood to the realities of life. Her family has been dining on its status as the descendants of conquistadors and they have the Alcántara coat-of-arms to prove it. Is status conferred through skin color, place of residence, family name, or connections to the government? Ana Isabel ponders and questions as she comes into contact with the various members of her community: the shoemaker, the teacher, the priest, the pharmacist, and the world of her very different grandfathers. The characters come to life through the narrator's distilled poetic descriptions and her evocation of their speech, clothing, and mannerisms. Through their interactions Palacios examines the racial attitudes of a Venezuela that was transitioning from a rural agrarian economy to an urban economy based on oil. The novel holds up a mirror to racial prejudices and reveals the social hierarchy that was based on skin color and other factors used in determining status and social standing. The importation of African slaves had had an enormous impact on the racial makeup of the country. Political affiliation and support of the current regime were becoming more important than established hierarchies based on lineage and landholding.

Ana Isabel: A Respectable Girl

The views of race and class in *Ana Isabel* reflect what Palacios heard and experienced. It was best to be "white on all four sides."

Ana Isabel is a sensitive and thoughtful child. She is aware of her surroundings and responds to the sights and smells and sounds all around her. She lives intensely. Her reality is revealed bit by bit as she confronts death, racial discrimination, anger, pain, social injustice and, finally, her transformation into adolescence and her resignation to the facts of life. Each chapter alternates with moments of joy and sadness; each chapter ends on a note of melancholy. As we last see Ana Isabel looking at her changing world, now trapped behind the bars of her window, we wonder what will become of her friends and family, and wish she had not stopped writing about it. Will the new generation usher in girls like Ana Isabel or is her character representative of a bygone era?

RoseAnna Mueller

Bibliography

Bustos Fernández, María José. "Ana Isabel, detrás de la reja: Identidad y procesos de subjetivación en *Ana Isabel, una niña decente*." *Escritura y desafío: Narradoras Venezolanas del siglo XX*. Eds. Edith Dimo and Amarilis Hidalgo de Jesús. Caracas: Monte Avila Editores, 1996. 181-189.

Bohórquez, Douglas. *Del costumbrismo a la vanguardia, la narrativa venezolana entre dos siglos*. Caracas: Monte Ávila Editores, 2007.

Homenaje a la memoria de Antonia Palacios y Juan Liscano. Caracas: Universidad Católica Andrés Bello, 2002.

Palacios, Antonia. *Ana Isabel, una niña decente*. Caracas: Monte Ávila Editores, 1969.

Pantin, Yolanda and Ana Teresa Torres. *El hilo de la voz. Antología crítica de escritoras venezolanas del siglo XX*. Caracas: Fundación Polar, 2003.

Liscano, Juan. "Prologo." *Ana Isabel, una niña decente*. Caracas: Monte Ávila Editores, 1977.

Palacios, Antonia. *Obras Completas*. Calicanto: Universidad Católica Andrés Bello, 1980.

Antonia Palacios: A Chronology

1904, 13 May - Antonia Isabel Palacios Caspers is born in Caracas. She is the daughter of Andrés Palacios and of Isabel Caspers, a friend of famous pianist Teresa Carreño.

1905 - The Palacios live in front of Plaza Candelaria.

1908 - Her brother Inocente is born. Juan Vicente Gómez seizes power and remains president or de facto ruler of Venezuela until 1935.

1911 - Antonia, who is being home-schooled by her mother, is taking French and piano lessons.

1914 - The Palacios move to Maiquetía, near Caracas.

1928 - Antonia Palacios and her brother become members of the so-called "Generation of 1928," a group protesting against Juan Vicente Gómez's repressive dictatorship.

1929 - She marries writer Carlos Eduardo Frías. She begins publishing in the magazine *Elite* under the pseudonym Mariana Ávila.

1935 - Her son Fernán is born.

1936 - In Paris, she studies the works of Piaget and Montessori.

1938 - She begins writing *Ana Isabel, una niña decente.*

1939 - She becomes secretary of the Agrupación Cultural Femenina and writes for the daily *Ahora.*

1940 - She serves as president of El Primer Congreso Venezolano de Mujeres (The First Congress of Venezuelan Women).

1941 - Her daughter Mariantonia Frías is born.

1944 - She publishes *París y tres recuerdos*, a book about the poets Aragón, Neruda and Vallejo.

1945 - She travels to Cuba with her husband, who invites Alejo Carpentier to join him in a PR firm, ARS Publicidad, (opened in 1946, it is still active today in Caracas).

1949 - *Ana Isabel, una niña decente* is first published in Buenos Aires by Editorial Losada. By 1950, the novel was being sold in Venezuela, Colombia, Argentina and other Latin American countries. In 1952 it reached Europe: Spain, Portugal, Holland and France.

1952 - Palacios begins writing *Viaje al Frailejón*, about a trip to the Andes. She and daughter Mariantonia, who is studying piano, go to live in New York City, so that Mariantonia could further her training.

1956-1958 - She lives in Paris with Mariantonia; in 1958 she audits classes at the Sorbonne and the College of France.

1960 - She returns to Venezuela.

1961 - She travels to Colombia.

1962 - *Ana Isabel* is published in Venezuela by Monte Ávila Editores. The novel is being read in many high schools in Venezuela. Her daughter Mariantonia marries Freddy Sánchez but she dies from diabetes ten months after their marriage.

1964 - First edition of *Crónica de las horas* is published.

1969 - Palacios begins having hearing problems.

1971 - She travels to Czechoslovakia, Hungary, Yugoslavia and Italy.

1972 - She publishes *Los insulares*.

1973 - She travels to Paris, London and Greece.

1975 - She travels to Argentina and New York.

1976 - She becomes the first woman to receive the Venezuelan National Prize for Literature.

1977 - She serves on the jury for Premio Rómulo Gallegos.

1978 - Her home, Calicanto, is a gathering place for literary meetings, a writing workshop and a laboratory for young writers to explore new forms of writing and expression. She encourages young writers and supported their efforts to bring new life into Venezuelan letters. Her role as a cultural disseminator cannot be under-estimated.

1984 - Her hearing problems lead to isolation.

1986 - Her husband Carlos Eduardo dies.

2001, 15 March - Antonia Palacios dies in Caracas. She is cremated and her ashes are scattered to the sea according to her wishes.

Ana Isabel: A Respectable Girl

To my children Fernán and Mariantonia,
to Carlos Eduardo, without whose encouragement
the young and timid Ana Isabel
would not have started on her way...

A. P.

Candelaria Town Square

na Isabel has always lived in front of a square. Those squares in Caracas that seem like small towns, surrounded by houses all pressed against each other. Houses all alike, all the same with their tiled eaves and bars across the windows. The windows are painted with oil paint. Rain and sun scorch the paint and Ana Isabel amuses herself by peeling off the paint to reveal the wood underneath. Those squares in Caracas overtaken by grass, with kapok trees, with overgrown fig trees, with dilapidated benches where sad, withered men sit. With little children who play Bogey Man, Cops and Robbers or Four Plants. With students who get up early and read their complicated textbooks by the yellow light of the city lamps. The Little Candelaria Square, a whole world in Ana Isabel's life! There is a little church in the little Candelaria Square. In the morning fog and at noon, when the sun falls perpendicular on the deserted square made larger in its loneliness, bells chime. In the afternoon the harsh ringing brass calls to prayer. Ana Isabel looks toward the window where Mrs. Alcántara's face appears.

"Ana Isabel, come in, it's already six o'clock."

Ana Isabel runs away pretending as if she hasn't heard. She crosses the smaller square in front of the church and heads to what she calls her hiding place. Ana Isabel's hiding place is the little alley behind the church. It's cold there. The tower doesn't let the sun shine in to warm the stones and the grass grows stunted there. The high wall forms a vault over the narrow street and the echo dims the voices. Ana Isabel feels small, very small, the walls are so high! And she tells herself it's a cave, a cave, a hideout for thieves, like Ali Baba's, or better yet, a cave where a fairy will come with her magic wand to change it into a palace. Ana Isabel sort of knows that fairies don't exist or if they do, you can't even see them, but she hopes that there will be one left behind and one day she'll show up, just for her. Ana Isabel fervently hopes for it, and doesn't tell anyone else about it. Lying on the cold stones she picks at the short grass. It's a dead-end alley through which hardly anyone passes. On one side is the broad wall of the church with its low door where the altar boy comes and goes. Ana Isabel knows him and talks to him every afternoon. He arrives wearing his sweaty tee-shirt and his threadbare trousers. His name is Pepe and he plays with the other children in the square who sometimes tug at his sleeve and shove him, laughing and shouting, "Altar boy, altar boy."

"C'mon. Leave me alone you'll make me drop the candles."

Because it's Pepe who brings the candles and the censer, balancing it and hitting his friend with it. He even lent it to Ana Isabel one afternoon. And how hard it was to balance it on the stones! Ana Isabel isn't intimidated by the altar boy. Sometimes she goes into the church with Estefanía and she feels like laughing, seeing Pepe so serious, dressed in red, with his lace tunic. Pepe passes close to her and winks at her. He carries a little plate with lots of centavos and lochas. What's the money for? One morning, during Mass, Estefanía made her leave, because Ana Isabel didn't know how to behave in church. Why does it make her laugh so much when the altar boy says: amen?

"The altar boy, Estefanía? But that's Pepe!"

The priest is another matter. This one does startle her and even frightens her a little. Besides, she's never seen him come in through the back door with a sweaty shirt or playing Bogey Man with the children in the square. In front of the church wall there is an empty lot where the wild scrub grows tall. Ana Isabel has never been there but she's seen it through a crack between two of the bricks. At the end of the street is Francisco the shoemaker's house. Francisco makes all kinds of repairs and replaces half-soles and puts taps on heels for the shoes of the entire neighborhood. Francisco's house is a miserable little hut painted blue. It doesn't have a hallway, the door is always open and Francisco can be seen sitting on a stool, working while he sings. A pile of old shoes is at his side. Twisted shoes, bent, missing buttons or laces... Shoes that "laugh alone," as the funny saying goes about shoes whose soles have come undone. Cheap shoes purchased with money saved up cent by cent, worn on Sundays to attend the outdoor band concerts or to take a ride on the trolley by El Paraíso, and when they are new, they are carried for blocks and blocks so they won't get dirty. Shoes that step on sharp rocks and get muddy when it rains when sewage runs through the dirt streets carrying with it empty cans and banana peels. The streets are always full of ragged children and dirty women hanging out by the doorways. Francisco's clients are very poor, but they wear shoes, at least on Sundays. Because there are some who wear alpargatas, and yet others who always go barefoot. Sometimes Francisco makes shoes for the ladies and Ana Isabel's mother had him put half-soles on her two-year old brown shoes that were still wearable. Next to Mrs. Alcántara's are the shoes of the coalman, the one who has a boy named Perico and a girl named Carmencita and another four who've "gone to heaven." Carmencita delivered her father's shoes and Ana Isabel looked on with envy because the other girl was given such an important task. It's true she had brought in Mrs. Alcántara's shoes, but she herself had been accompanied by Estefanía, while Carmencita had done it all by herself like a grownup. Besides, Carmencita doesn't have anyone to go with her and she doesn't go to school like Ana Isabel does, she doesn't even know her alphabet; but she goes to the corner store and buys three cents worth of butter and two cents worth of brown sugar. Carmencita doesn't play much and that's why Ana Isabel thinks she always looks so sad with her little smudged face and her two braids so tangled up they look like they've never been combed, although they must have, because Ana Isabel has seen her on Sundays with her hair very smoothed out with coconut oil and with two red ribbons tied to the ends of her braids, holding hands with Perico who's also cleanly dressed and wearing new alpargatas. Ana Isabel and Jaime see them when they go to visit their cousins the Izaguirres and Ana Isabel follows them with her eyes until they are out of sight. Ana Isabel would rather go with them to fly kites up on Sarría hill instead of having to go visit the Izaguirres and visit with Josefina who talks only about her dresses and her piñata parties where she and Jaime aren't invited to because they are so poor, according to Josefina.

Francisco hammers away with his mouth full of nails. He's putting a tap on the heel of Amelia's shoes. Amelia is the one who carries water up the hill and sells it for a *locra* a can. "Those people up on the hill are so lazy!" Amelia says. They live up there, in the slums, where at night a dim light glows, like another star. During January's cold, lying down on the hard earth, drinking only *guarapo* and eating casabe. And they are thin, very thin, those people up on the hill. The children have big stomachs stretched tight like drums. "But they are so lazy!" says Amelia. Ana Isabel puts her ears against the stones to feel them vibrate when Francisco hammers. At times, there are big and long silences and Ana Isabel looks up at the sky where the stars are beginning to shine. The bells toll.

"Ana Isabel. Where are you? Just look at this girl who's always hanging out here. Your mother is hoarse from shouting at you to come in, girl." The old black woman's silhouette is outlined against the mild June sky. The crickets sing in the empty lot...

Two Funerals

na Isabel runs to the room. She locks the door, closes the shutters and total darkness fills the room. Throwing herself down, her head between her arms, with her face on the cement, she cries. Jaime wanted to comfort her, but Ana Isabel ran into the room, screaming and shouting.

"Leave her alone, my son, she wants to be alone. Let her be."

A heavy black cloud hides the sun. The bougainvillea in the patio turns a muted red. The little fish stopped swirling around and formed a little group, shivering under the water. From the mouth of the Cupid made of cement, a small trickle of water emerges and forms ripples on the tranquil surface of the fountain's basin. In the Alcántara household, in the shadows of the room, Ana Isabel weeps in a soft, faint lament, almost a whisper.

"Jaime, little brother, how bad I am to you!"

Why is she bad? Why does she feel like punching, biting? Is she like her father? Could she be? Ana Isabel shudders. If she's like her father when she's grown up she'll be like him. And she'll be bad like him. Although he's often kind and affectionate towards them, with Ana Isabel and Jaime.

"Come here and ride this horse, Ana Isabel!" With a leap, Ana Isabel climbs onto her father's knees and he dandles her up and down on his legs as he sings:

When I rode to the plains
* Orí, orí, orí, oríon*
Galloping on my little horse...

Yes, at those times her father is good and she knows he loves her and she throws her thin little arms around his neck.

9

"I love you very much, daddy."

But Ana Isabel hides her face to keep her father from kissing her. Her father's breath is harsh and metallic and his mustache is sharp and it scratches her. Ana Isabel runs her hand across her face. Why does her face hurt? Oh, yes! Her father's hand! That big, bony hand with the enormous knuckles. Ana Isabel runs her hand against her forehead and feels her swollen skin. Maybe it was the ring. The heavy thick gold ring with the Alcántara coat of arms her father always wears. How many times has Ana Isabel had the Alcántara coat of arms explained to her? Without a doubt it's the coat of arms that struck her. It sure strikes hard, that Alcántara coat of arms! And Ana Isabel feels a silent rage drying her tears. A dark rage surfaced from the depths, the very depths of her being. Against her house, the house of the Alcántaras! with its rigid ancestors in their worm-eaten frames. Against her mother's tame and serene resignation. Against her father... Oh, her father! Rage and hatred, a great childish and confused hatred...

"I want to die! I want to die!"

What, die? Yes, to die. That would be her best revenge. To die!

There will be long silences in the Alcántara household, so long that you can hear the drops of water falling on the tranquil surface of the fountain. Hurried footsteps will cross the patio and arrive at the room's door.

"Ana Isabel, Ana Isabel, open up!" No one answers. They will force the door open. The lock will fall down on the cement with a loud crash and her mother will call out, "She's dead! She's dead! Oh, my God!" And her father, trembling, will approach with his eyes wide open.

"It was my fault," he will exclaim. "I killed her. It was my fault. It's me who killed her."

And the house will fill with shouts and cries and no one will hear her little brother's sobs, who doesn't even want to look at her...

10

Two Funerals

The old black woman, old Estefanía will shout hoarsely, "My little girl, my little girl! Who killed her?" And even Gregoria, who never cries, will wipe away a tear with the corner of her apron. On hearing all the shouting, Vicente, the servant next door, will come running with Chucuto following behind. Chucuto will look at her with his sad eyes and will lick her hand, and she, Ana Isabel, will lie cold and stretched out on the cement floor. And they will all plan a beautiful funeral! With a big, white carriage! The horses will be caparisoned and will have big white feathers on their heads. Men wearing dark suits with gold buttons will carry heavy silver candelabras on their shoulders. The sputtering candle flames will light up the ivory cross. And the wreaths, many wreaths. There will be so many that even Aunt Clara's room will smell like lilies. And how many lilies?...

Eight, nine, ten, eleven...

Eleven, like the funeral for Miss Ercilia, the minister's sister. Ercilia Fajardo. Ana Isabel always saw her on her way to church, Miss Ercilia, with her black hair parted down the middle, straight and symmetrical, peeking out of the folds of her hood. Miss Ercilia who spent her life in church and gave lots of money to the priest. It was she who offered the statue of the Virgin silk robes and brilliant gems. "She's a saint, a true saint," said the priest as he joined his hands together, "a saint from the plains..." Because the Fajardos came from the plains and don Celestino was the General's friend. Don Celestino Fajardo, Miss Ercilia's brother.

"Yes, they are nobodies, Federico," Mrs. Alcántara used to comment. "Years ago they went barefoot and now they put on airs. All you need is to have money and to be in the good graces of the General..." Years ago they went barefoot through the great wide fields. Miss Ercilia didn't have those symmetrical tresses inside the folds of her hood, because she didn't wear a cloak under the breezes of the

11

plains, but she had two heavy black braids that fell to her shoulders and sometimes she pinned a bright red flower to them. And she had a suitor, Miss Ercilia, a plainsman like herself, thin and jaunty, who sang verses to her that floated on the broad, mild dusk. But the suitor died of a fever. One always dies of fevers on the plains. Miss Ercilia grew pale and thin. Don Celestino was named minister and the family went back to the capital. In Caracas, Miss Ercilia left the house only to go to church, each time thinner, each time paler. Her braids came apart and in their place were those straight, symmetrical tresses. It was a lovely funeral, that of the minister's sister. Ana Isabel had seen it on the way home from school. The streets were full of people and the police didn't let anyone through until the funeral procession had passed by. Apparently, the General was there, among the attendants. Ana Isabel had stopped near the baker, who had left his basket of bread on the ground. A woman was shouting to be let through because her daughter was ill and would die without having seen her. But the police formed an impassable unified barricade. On the corner a little boy was crying because he wanted to eat a lollipop. The candy seller held his agave pole bristling with red and yellow candies upon which hungry flies would land... "Be quiet, my son. I don't have the centavos to buy candy with. Let me hold you up. Come so you can see the funeral. Look son at that pile of wreaths!" And the landaus, eight, nine, ten, eleven. And such a big house!"

Ana Isabel knew her even though she wasn't friends with the Minister's daughter Cristina. She had been there with Cristina's cousin, Cecilia, who was going to get some used dresses that she had promised to give her. Cecilia entered alone, leaving the door ajar and Ana Isabel drew close to peer into the house. What a big house! All decorated with mosaic tiles. Even the patio, instead of having plants, had mosaic tiles. Not even one guava plant, not even a begonia, not even one flower. And the minister is so rich. Ana Isabel thinks about what she's often heard her father say.

"He's a thief, Ana, a thief and a scoundrel. A genuine scoundrel."

"Good heavens, Federico! According to you, everyone's a thief, only the Alcántaras seem honorable to you."

"No sir, I'm telling you he's a scoundrel who made a fortune stealing sacks of cement."

Sacks of cement? Ana Isabel doesn't understand how you can steal sacks of cement. Where would you hide them? It's true that the patio was big, but it's sad and bare. No fountain in the middle, no ferns, not one green leaf... Sacks of cement? Where would he hide them?

"Step away, step away the funeral procession is coming through!"

The police shove the people and one woman tripped and fell on the baker's basket. The loaves of bread rolled around on the ground and the children pounced on them and started running away.

How many landaus? Eight, nine, ten, eleven... Yes, eleven. Ana Isabel had counted them.

A funeral like the minister's sister's... Because Ana Isabel had seen another funeral. That day, the streets were deserted. Four men, surrounded by children carried a small white box, as small as Ana Isabel. The men were thin and their faces were sweaty. Two rotting hibiscus flowers were tied to the box with a piece of string.

"What's that?" Ana Isabel had asked?

"A funeral."

"A funeral without carriages and wreaths?"

"Yes, child, a funeral for the poor..."

And then Gregoria had added, "They're taking that one to the boneyard. Just the same as kings. Everybody going to the same place, whites and blacks, rich and poor.

Over there, everybody same..."

Ana Isabel started to tremble. "Over there everyone's the same..."

Now she doesn't want to die. If she's going to be like Gregoria now Ana Isabel doesn't want to die. She doesn't want to be like Gregoria, with her watery eyes, reddened by smoke, and with those hands... Oh, Gregoria's hands! With their ragged nails and swollen veins and a big blackened finger on account of washing so much laundry. If she's going to be like Gregoria now Ana Isabel doesn't want to die...

The sun is fading from the patio, climbing up the red tiled roofs of the whitewashed walls. The water trickles slowly, continuously. In the Alcántara household, where silence reigns. Ana Isabel has fallen asleep on the cold cement, in the darkness of the room.

Carnival Sunday

na Isabel smoothes her little red skirt with the black bands and flattens out the little white apron with her hands. "Who's ugly now!" Ana Isabel's little sharp face is resplendent. Her cheeks are rouged and her eyes are shining. The straight hair is gathered up high on her head with a big black ribbon because Ana Isabel is dressed up as an Alsatian village girl. "I dare them to say who's ugly…" Ana Isabel gazes at herself in the mirror. Here comes Jaime. Jaime looks like a prince, with his wool trousers and his lace waistcoat. How handsome, how extremely handsome her brother looks! Ana Isabel feels her heart suddenly clench… But she's not ugly. The Bermúdez family hasn't seen her in her costume, that's why only her brother was invited.

"Why don't you send the little boy over? So handsome, so sweet, the little boy…"

But Mrs. Alcántara hadn't sent him over. "What a strange thing for those people to ask, to invite just Jaime!"

Without a doubt, the Bermúdez family hasn't seen her dressed up like an Alsatian girl. Ana Isabel looks at herself in the mirror once more and rearranges the ribbon on her head. There will be dancing in the little Candelaria Square. Folk dancing. Mrs. Alcántara has warned Estefanía to be careful and to not pass across the square.

"Those common people, Estefanía, they are so rude and they might jostle the children and mess up their costumes." Those costumes were so hard to come up with! Ana Isabel's had been the easiest one. Two meters of red satin and some black ribbon and the skirt was done. But the ribbon! For the ribbon Mrs. Alcántara had thrown thrift out the window. It had to be stiff so it would keep its shape up high on her head. Mrs. Alcántara sewed wire around the edges to keep it stiff, like that, stiff and high on Ana Isabel's straight, golden hair. It was lucky that Jaime could use the old trousers of her nephew German's. And the lace? The lovely lace? Didn't it come from Ana Isabel's first mantilla, the mantilla her grandmother gave her? Ah! The good old days. Mrs. Alcántara's eyes were dim from sewing. That lace was filled with memories for her.

"All right, then, so you know, be careful and do as Estefanía tells you."

"Yes, Mommy."

"Give us your blessing, Mommy, give us your blessing, Daddy..."

"Just a minute, Estefanía. Only just a tiny minute more..."

"Holy Jesus, what's with this girl, always making me do what I don't want to..."

And now old Estefanía is crossing the square with Ana Isabel and Jaime. How festive the little Candelaria Square looks! Ana Isabel hardly recognizes it. All festooned, with crepe-paper strips of a thousand colors, red, blue, green, yellow... And how many things there are for sale! Here, the arepa stand, such spongy arepas, that Domitila fried up, the same one who delivers arepas to their house every day. La Negra Domitila is wearing makeup and she's covered with black and red necklaces. Two big hoops hang from La Negra Domitila's ears, who's laughing, with her white teeth showing, near the steaming pot.

"I want an arepa, Estefanía..."

"Stop this nonsense, girl. Remember what your mother said... Walk faster and don't stop so often, or we'll never get across this blessed square!"

But La Negra Estefanía also stops. How she remembers her younger days, La Negra Estefanía, when she moved her feet, her firm black flesh, without missing a beat, La Negra Estefanía. Ah, black woman! Ah, what a spicy black woman!

There is a guarapo stand and further another one offering carato in bottles topped off with half an orange.

Ana Isabel would like to drink the sweet corn drink from the bottle, like everyone else around the stand but she doesn't dare ask Estefanía. Next to the statue they are playing a waltz. Which one? "Eva's Waltz."

Da da da da, da, da...

Where are Ana Isabel and Jaime heading? To their cousins the Izaguirres' house to watch the parade go by...

It's a pity Ana Isabel is a respectable girl. There in the square there are also other children, but they are not respectable... Ana Isabel doesn't like her cousins the Izaguirres. Josefina doesn't play because she's afraid of getting dirty, or messing up her dress, she only likes to play with dolls. True, she has a big doll house that Ana Isabel covets, but she doesn't like to run and jump like Ana Isabel, or climb up on the roof or to the top of the mango tree. And Luis? Ana Isabel is afraid of her cousin Luis because he's always whispering dirty things to her. Of course Ana Isabel has a terrible urge to these hear bad things, but she's afraid to, because God might punish her.

"Ana Isabel, look at the little donkey. The little donkey is dancing, let's go see it," and Jaime hangs onto his sister's arm.

"Holy Jesus, these kids just won't stand still."

But La Negra Estefanía shakes her head without conviction. Her feet are planted on the square's cement floor, and she's all eyes, her eyes are wide open as she looks at the wide ruffled skirt, the donkey's head decorated with paper roses, the shaking maracas and the singing folk singer. The little donkey frightens Ana Isabel a little. While it's dancing, all is well. She looks at the donkey's head marking time and she listens to the maracas that send happy shivers through her body. But, when the dance is over, the donkey huskily clears its throat and picks up its skirt to reveal feet, a man's feet, big and dirty, wearing worn-out alpargatas...

In the square, the music is deafening, couples jostle each other, and Ana Isabel and Jaime, clinging to old Estefanía's skirt, can't continue on their way, held back by a human tide dancing and tapping its feet. An acrid smell, a smell of onions and sweat, the stench of liquor. A smell of coconut oil and cheap perfume and dirty alpargatas rises up from the couples pushing and bumping about. Steam escapes from the arepa stand and mixes with the smell of ordinary grease and the acrid smell of the dancing crowd. Ana Isabel doesn't like that smell. She feels dizzy... Now she doesn't want to be in the square, with the dressed-up children. Now, she would rather go to her cousins the Izaguirres' house to watch the parade go by.

"Look at Pepe, Ana Isabel! There's Pepe!" Pepe! How could it be that she hadn't recognized the altar boy? He's disguised as an apache dancer, with a red kerchief tied around his neck and a charcoal mustache above his thick lips.

"Look, Ana Isabel, and Vicente, too!"

Vicente, a pair of red horns swaying on his head. Vicente, with his painted face, disguised as the devil. He hasn't seen Ana Isabel and Jaime. He's dancing, wearing a cape. Vicente's arms fold the sides of the cape tightly around his hips. He curls it up, presses his arms together, presses his arms...

"Hey, there, my black woman, hey there!"

Ana Isabel has never seen him like this. Vicente, who's always so serious!

18

Two Funerals

"Good-bye, Estefanía. Good bye black woman..."

Wow, look at Nemesio, what a dancer! Ana Isabel didn't recognize Nemesio, the baker, either. What a dancer! Nemesio's feet have been dancing since Saturday.

"I'm delivering your bread today, ma'am, because I won't be back until Monday." And they all said the same thing: the mailman, the coal man, the butcher... All of them. They all said the same thing. All those who are bent over under the weight of their burdens. Those who rise at dawn, shivering from the cold, with barely two gulps of cane juice in their stomachs. Those who work with their hands, with their feet, with their crooked backs. Those who work with their hands. Hands with calluses and blisters. Hands with broken, missing nails. Hands from which bread, milk, coal and meat and cheese pass through. Hands that grind. Hands that wring laundry. Hands that chop down trees and saw wood. Hands that work the soil and build houses, squares, schools.

And here they all are, this Carnival Sunday afternoon, with their painted faces, their brightly-colored kerchiefs, their tattooed arms. There they are with their necklaces, hats, trinkets. With their laughter and shouting...

"Hey, there, my black woman! What a saucy black woman!"

There they are on that Carnival Sunday, forgetting their mud huts, their ill-smelling clothes, their withered faces...

The coal man's children, Perico and Carmencita start climbing up the greased pole. How shiny and how high! Up at the top is a five bolivar piece. Let's see who can climb to the top... But the coal man isn't worried about his children today. Carmencita is dressed up like a flower, with a costume made out of red and green crepe paper. And Perico is wearing a ruffled collar and is dressed up like a

19

clown. But the coal man isn't concerned about his children today. He's dancing and his eyes are shining and when he laughs, his breath smells bad...

Someone pushed Carmencita and she started crying. Perico takes her hand and leads her to the arepa stand. Domitila already gave her one, round and golden and her eyes are smiling through her tears.

"There goes Amelia!"

"Bye, Amelia!"

"Olé, for the Spanish lady!"

"Look at that blonde!..."

"Careful you don't break it, girl."

The music keeps playing without ceasing. It vibrates, pulsates, through legs, hips. Hips that sway, that rock, feet that sweep the ground because a joropo is playing. The bodies sweat, they push against each other, they part, they turn around with upraised arms and meet again amidst shouts and the snapping of fingers. The strong, acrid smell of the crowd rises, rises up to the flowering hummingbird tree, up to the church steeple with its muted bells, the strong acrid smell of the crowd.

"See here, boy, where is Ana Isabel?"

"Ana Isabel!"

"Just a minute ago she was right here... Where is she?"

"Ana Isabel! Ana Isabel!"

Ana Isabel doesn't hear Jaime's shouts, or the old black woman's cries.

The crowd is turning, dancing, sweating, singing, laughing, shouting, whoa there, my black woman. What a saucy black woman!

The crowd lifts her, shakes her, pushes her. And there goes Ana Isabel, pushed, shoved, squeezed, dragged along by the wild force. There goes Ana Isabel, in her little red skirt with the black ribbon stripes, with her little white apron and the big ribbon high up on her golden hair. There goes Ana Isabel, tiny, lost, between the mighty power of the crowd. The acrid odor surrounds her, enfolds her... But Ana Isabel doesn't feel nauseous; she closes her eyes and allows herself to move along, pushed along by the current that drags her who knows where.

Her feet barely touch the ground. Could Ana Isabel be dreaming? Is she telling herself stories? The stories she tells herself at night, in her little warm bed, close to her pillow so soft. But where is the fairy? And the magic wand? And the prince? The enchanted prince who is going to take her up through the clouds on his winged horse? And the mighty force grows, grows and surrounds little Ana Isabel even more.

But Ana Isabel isn't afraid. Why isn't she afraid? Those people are so common... so vulgar...

And her mother's voice sounds so far away. And the house is so far away, the sunny patio, the steaming bowl of soup, and her bed, so soft...

The Map of Venezuela

*L*uisa Figueroa, Esperanza Caldera, Justina Ferbau, Celestina Guillén, Ana Isabel Alcántara...

"And now," the teacher says, "Let's copy down the list of what you need to buy for the dresses. One must be careful when choosing the fabric, so it's of the best quality. Don't forget that, along with yourselves, the group from the Sister's High School will also be there, and our dresses must not be inferior to theirs. Let's see, write: white linen batiste, four meters..."

While she is dictating, the teacher delicately poises on her chair, and she raps her ruler on the table. When she talks a lot, the teacher blushes and her eyes, sunken and watery, shine as though she had a fever. She is thin and a little hunchbacked. Her skin is dry, and when she gets angry a rosy rash appears on her neck. It's ten thirty. Classes will be over at eleven. In the room the girls are hurriedly writing. It's a bright and spacious room. In the middle of it a door opens up to the patio and at the end there is a hallway that leads to the stairs to the laundry room. The floor is made of wood and it echoes with the girls' footsteps. The desks are painted a dark color. Old desks, full of nicks and scratches with marks from discarded penknives and splinters and big ink stains. On either side of the wall the hooks hold piqué caps and hats.

"Valenciennes lace, two pieces. The wreath you'll need to buy at the French Company, just in from Paris." The teacher dictates in a steady, monotonous voice, as though she has been reciting from memory, while she continues to balance herself delicately in the chair. Luisa Figueroa moistens her pencil with her saliva each time she writes down a word. She's the same age as Ana Isabel, but she's shorter and thinner. Luisa Figueroa hardly ever speaks to Ana Isabel and always looks at her with an air of compassion. One day, Ana Isabel found her in the hallway whispering and hugging Esperanza Caldera. They were whispering and started to giggle when they saw her. As she approached them, she heard her father's name. Why were they talking about her father, and why were they laughing? Cecilia Guillén sits on one side of Ana Isabel and on the other side is Justina Ferbau. Justina Ferbau is Catalan and her mother owns a beauty shop and a store and she sells "pretty things," as Justina Ferbau says. "Madrices a Marrón" has a big display window with gold letters: "Madame Ferbau." Ladies' hairstyles are always shown with their smooth curls, just so, in the display case. But Ana Isabel's eyes follow something else. That red patent leather belt with a painted clock that always reads four thirty! They come in white, green and yellow. Justina's was white, and Ana Isabel had passed her hand softly over that clock that always read four thirty. But the red one! Ana Isabel pressed her face against the glass while she gazed on it... Ana Isabel had never been to Justina's house. "A Catalan!" exclaimed Mrs. Alcántara. "Who knows what kind of people they are." "But they aren't black, mama." Justina was not black. Her skin was white and rosy. Her golden hair fell in curls to her shoulders, her eyes were blue, her hands were plump and dimpled.

"It's best not to get too friendly with those people. Who knows what kind of people they are!..." And so that was that, she'd never visited in Justina's house. But several times she'd gone into the house looking for notebooks that Justina offered her and she had approached the living room whose windows faced the street. Belts, caps, baby clothes, fabric flowers. Poppies and pale roses. Mrs. Ferbau was always behind the counter, with her hair swept up in a thick bun on the top of her head. She wore a corset, white muslin blouses and a grey wool skirt. She herself worked as the clerk and she recorded the day's sales in a thick book. Ana Isabel was in awe of Mr. Ferbau. Justina told fabulous stories about him, of voyages and storms on the high seas when her father lifted her high in his arms as the waves swept the deck. His eyes were blue, just like Justina's, and he had black hair and a mustache. One day, Ana Isabel saw him lifting Justina high up in his arms so she could reach with her fingertips the lamp surrounded by a porcelain shade that hung from the ceiling in the middle of the salon. Ana Isabel wished he could do the same thing to her, so she could close her eyes and pretend it was the sea and she could feel the waves sweeping the deck...

"Write faster, girls, it's almost eleven o'clock. Mother-of-pearl buttons, two dozen..."

It's Wednesday. Geography class. The teacher has taken half an hour out of class time so the girls can make the list. The map of Venezuela is spread against the whitewashed wall and displays its islands, its oceans, its colors. There is the green section of Monagas State, and the salmon-colored one is Guárico State, and the little blue one, circled in gray, is Valencia Lake and up high is Maracaibo, Maracaibó, the Indians shouted. The yellow mountains climb up towards the snowy peaks. The black lines of the rivers cross each other. The Orinoco, Meta, Motatán, Apure and Caroní run like silver lightning. They water the wide lands, some are left behind, some among cornfields and others with their deep, dark voices hurl themselves into the sea. The blue grows bigger and expands, spilling over and marking off Venezuela's territory. The Caribbean breaks on the rocky shores, against the gentleness of warm sands. The map of Venezuela! Ana Isabel caresses it as she studies it. How many times has she traced it with her hands, lines, shadows, colors! Here is a brown curve, there the hollowed out of unexpected mountains whose audacious and harsh peaks penetrate the waters. She knows the names by heart. Choroní, the salty land of coconut trees. Barlovento, the black land of black people and cacao. Santa Lucía, where the breeze makes the sugar cane sway and moan. Ortiz, desolate and empty... And if we were to travel inland? Who knows the thousand roads of the plains? How many times, with her little finger, has Ana Isabel traced the vast coast of Venezuela? From the gulf of Paria, from Cristóbal Colón towards the Río Caribe and the slender trail that buries itself in the sea: Manicuare. To the right, Cumana, Barcelona, Boca de Uchire. And jumping to the far end, Punta Cumarebo, on the very top of the jellyfish of Paraguaná, and that yellow bit that falls on the blue Caribbean, the Goagira peninsula. Wide Venezuelan coast that follows the voice of the ocean, filled with the breath of the ocean and the salty winds that scatter its sands. Tip of Araya, white in the sun, white with salt! Chichiriviche. Tucacas, Tocuyo on the coast... And...the sea... Always the sea! It comes and goes, sings, waves, shakes, next to Venezuela's immense coast. What can the bottom of the sea be like? There where the light fades and the cold waters meet the dark abyss. Among fish, among algae, submerged among the greens and reds, the buried tree, the root, the spikes, the bodies of buried children and women with their hair forever tangled by manes of eternal hair. What light! What silence, oh, immense silence. Quiet down there at the bottom of the sea. Motionless arms, legs, they can be seen on the bottom, the keels of the ships that plow the waters, above, where men speak and gesture. To go down to the bottom of the sea!

"Cecilia, would you like to go to the bottom of the sea?"

"What's with you, Ana Isabel! To the bottom of the sea? What for?"

"To see the color..."

"But you've never been to the sea, Ana Isabel!"

It's true, she's never been to the sea, but it's easy to imagine it...

"What's the sea like, Cecilia?"

Cecilia is silent for a minute as she twirls a chestnut curl around her finger.

"The sea," she says, as though she's emerging from a faraway place. "The sea? It's a sky that moves."

"A sky that moves? With clouds and stars? An immense blue sky that stretches from side to side and falls to earth."

"A candle worth four reales..."

"I can't hear you, Miss." Esperanza Caldera calls out in her strident voice.

"A four-reale candle," the teacher patiently repeats.

Cecilia Guillén whispers in Ana Isabel's ear, "Four reales for a candle! My mother won't buy it for me. That dress is going to cost a lot of money."

The school clock slowly allows eleven to strike.

"Eleven! It's eleven o'clock, Miss." The lids of the desk come down with a bang. The girls push each other, grabbing the corners of each other's aprons.

"Leave me alone. I'm telling the teacher you're pushing me."

"Always a tattletale!"

"Silence girls, silence!"

"See you this afternoon, Miss. See you this afternoon."

"See you this afternoon."

The classroom is deserted. The teacher sits at her table, looking over the empty desks and empty benches. Dark curly clouds reach up to the sky. A gust of rain pounds against the window and lifts up the edges of the map of Venezuela.

The Kiskadee

"No, my dear daughter. You won't be able to receive your First Holy Communion. You know that I'd let you if I could. I would, but that dress is very expensive and we are very poor. Don't cry Ana Isabel. Why are you crying? You'll receive your First Communion by yourself. I'll fix up your white dress, the one with the pleats, I'll put on a new collar and a wide satin sash with a big bow. You like that? Come here, my little one... But don't cry, Ana Isabel. There's no point in crying over a dress. Don't leave. Where are you going?"

Ana Isabel has started running. Away! She wants to go away. Where? She doesn't know. Away. Far away... Far from home. The Alcántara home. To run through the fields, the mountains, along the riversides... But, where can she go, little Ana Isabel with her little pale face and her eight fragile years? Her chest cannot hold the urge to get away, to go who knows where, to be free. Free? But what's keeping her captive? She could run away one night when everyone is asleep. One night, when the tree in the little square is deep in shadows and seems so tall it reaches the sky. A moonless night when the little ragged children are asleep in the doorways. She could run away one night when everyone's asleep. She'd head towards Gamboa on foot. Walking along the white path in the dark of night. Walking... She'd lie down on the grass to rest. She'd awaken to the cackle of guacarachas and she would stretch out her arms and legs and would laugh out loud on finding herself free, stretched out on the grass, on the road to Gamboa.

Why doesn't Ana Isabel leave one night, some night when everyone's asleep? Ana Isabel has climbed up to the roof. From there she can see the treetops in the square and Otilia's yard.

27

If only she could live in the treetops!

I'll fix up your white dress, the one with the pleats...

Ana Isabel doesn't want to cry. It's true she climbed to the top of the roof so she can cry in peace. Because she doesn't want the others to see her crying. Yes, that's why she's here, so she can have a good cry and feel miserable!

But she's not crying, Ana Isabel. The leaves in the trees are so green! On top of the guasimo tree there's a kiskadee with its fine little claws and its yellow breast shining among the branches.

"How vain!" Aunt Clara had said. "To cry like that over a dress. A girl who's about to become the Lord's betrothed. "The Lord's betrothed? Ana Isabel had not thought about that. She was dreaming of the veil, and the rose wreath just in from Paris, like the teacher said. And her portrait, as she knelt on a kneeler, with her hands folded in prayer, her eyes gazing upwards, like the one she'd seen in the window of "Martinez Photography." Let's see, if Luisa Figueroa and Esperanza Caldera would dare to call her ugly after seeing that portrait...

"The Lord's betrothed!" Why hadn't the teacher mentioned this?

"You have to be careful when choosing the fabric, it has to be of the best quality. A group from the Sister's School will be receiving their First Communion with you..."

The teacher never mentioned they were going to marry the Lord. Oh, no! Ana Isabel doesn't want that. Won't she ever marry? Of course! But it will be to a prince who owns a big gold and marble palace. She will be a princess and Luisa Figueroa and Esperanza Caldera will be her vassals. Yes, she is going to marry a prince... She could also marry a sailor. Ana Isabel has never been to the sea. All her friends have been to Macuto and Maiquetia on vacation, but they've never taken her along.

"It's impossible, my little daughter. Vacations are for the rich. The poor are condemned to stay put..."

But Ana Isabel loved the sea, just like she loved the things she dreamed about... Yes, she'll marry a sailor, like one of those who've arrived in Caracas on a steamship that's anchored off LaGuiara. With their red and blue striped tee-shirts and their broad shoulders. It's true that their tee-shirts were dirty and sweaty tee-shirts and the sailor's faces looked sad and tired. But Ana Isabel is thinking only of the sea breezes and how the waves must look, high and green, perhaps...

The Lord's betrothed. If she has to marry the Lord then Ana Isabel doesn't want to receive her First Communion. The Lord is so good, the teacher constantly repeats. But the Lord sees everything Ana Isabel does. His eyes are everywhere and when she is bad, the Lord punishes her. And he is merciless and doesn't forgive anyone anything...

The Lord, who is so good...

But it's the Lord who allowed her father to get sick, and made them poor, so poor that she hasn't ever been to the sea...the sea, one of the Lord's creations. He gives money, however, to those who steal, like don Celestino Fajardo, who steals sacks of cement, while her father, who is more honorable than anyone, for doesn't he belong to one of the most honorable families of Venezuela? Cauldrons of gold on a field of blue! Her father, Dr. Alcántara, is always sick and he wears worn-out shoes. God created the sun, the moon, the stars...and all of lovely and sad Venezuela. And little thin, naked children and Gregoria blowing on the stove with her watery eyes and her blackened finger and her big round nail. The poor were made to suffer. To suffer and bear it... Has the Lord created the poor for them to bear it? But why? My Lord? So then, why don't they steal like don Celestino Fajardo, so then they can buy themselves a big house all made of tiles and eat strawberries with milk, just like Cecilia says about Cristina, the minister's daughter?

Why don't the poor steal?

If the poor stole, that would be the end of the poor.

Everyone would be rich. Everyone would be happy and God wouldn't punish anyone, like don Celestino, who lives so happily.

Kiskadee! Kiskadee!

The kiskadee started singing. He's perched on a delicate branch and happily balances himself. Ana Isabel looks at his little round eyes and his brown head.

If the poor stole, that would be the end of the poor. Everyone would have a big house. Perico and Carmencita wouldn't be living in that small dark hut. Pepe the altar boy wouldn't have to lie down on the black dirt, in the San José de Avila slum. She had seen it herself, one day when she went there to fly a kite... Pepe had let her into his house. Ana Isabel looked all over and saw only bare hard earth and a woman who kept coughing. That day Mrs. Alcántara scolded Estefanía for allowing Ana Isabel to go to that dirty slum.

"Those slums, Estefanía, where you can only catch diseases and bad habits."

If everyone was rich! If everyone was rich, she would go to the sea. They would buy her a long candle and the rose wreath and every day she could eat a big bowl of strawberries with milk.

Kiskadee! Kiskadee!

When the kiskadee sings, it's about to rain. But the sky is blue. Not one dark cloud.

Ana Isabel has taken off her shoes so she can walk on the roof without breaking the tiles. She wants to see what the weather is like in the slums of Petare. It's clear in Petare. The sky is a whitewashed blue, now that the sun is setting. A warm breeze blows across the red tiles, a soft breeze that lulls her to sleep. Ana Isabel is dreaming... If everyone was rich, it would put an end to the poor.

It would be the end of the poor...

Confession

The classroom lies in shadow. The teacher closed the window so the rain wouldn't get in. The tall Royal Palm in the patio sways in the wind and is wet from the rain, a heavy rain that falls in big drops over the earth. The girls are quiet. It's the first day of the retreat. First day of the retreat! How she had awakened that first day of the retreat! Awakened? But she had hardly slept! Chucuto was howling sadly all night and Ana Isabel, with her eyes wide open, was shivering under the sheets. Just as the sun began to shine weakly on the patio she managed to get to sleep. But then her mother's voice made her jump up. "Ana Isabel, get up, you have to be at school by seven. The retreat starts today, don't you remember?" Of course she remembered! All night long she had thought of nothing but. Three days! Three days during which she would arrive at the high school at seven in the morning and stay there till seven at night. Ana Isabel's hands are cold with excitement. During catechism class Father Mayorca had talked about the retreat a lot.

"Three days to quiet your minds and pray and be in full contact with the Lord." That's what Father Mayorca had said. Ana Isabel is afraid of the "contact with the Lord" Father Mayorca talks about. Surely no one may talk, or sing, or laugh... "You're going to be late. What a disobedient girl!"

"Disobedient?"

To disobey is a sin, a mortal sin, Father Mayorca said. Mortal sin! She'd have to tell it to the priest. And the terror Ana Isabel feels about confessing, even if the teacher taught the girls all about it. Sitting on a low chair she played the part of the priest with Ana Isabel kneeling next to her.

"Recite the Act of Contrition."

"I, a sinner, confess to God..."

Ana Isabel's thin voice was almost a whisper.

"Now tell your sins..."

But, did she have to tell the teacher those terrible things? No, Ana Isabel can't do it. How many bad things had Ana Isabel thought about the teacher? How many times had she lied to her? And why should she say what Justina told her? The big secret Ana Isabel keeps deep down inside since the day Justina told her that babies don't come from Paris. Justina made her swear she wouldn't tell anyone, anyone, and Ana Isabel solemnly swore as she crossed her fingers saying, "I swear." And the urge Ana Isabel has that Cecilia tell her "bad things" like the kisses her sister Amalia gives her boyfriend Pedro Ladera? Will she have to tell about all this? And...also what her cousin Luis told her? Ana Isabel started to tremble. What her cousin Luis told her she could tell no one, least of all Father Mayorca when it's time to confess.

"Hiding a sin is the worst of all sins. To keep a sin in secret is a sacrilege."

Ana Isabel doesn't know exactly what a sacrilege is, but Father Mayorca said that whoever commits it will go to hell for an eternity.

Eternity! What's eternity like? It will be days and days and more days, nights and more nights. Trees will wither away and other trees will grow. Houses will collapse and other houses will be built and other birds will be born and new flowers will grow. All her friends will die and other girls will come to receive their First Communions. And there will be other skies and other stars... Chucuto will have died, but another little dog that won't be named Chucuto will be there. And Carmencita and Perico won't be there. The coal man will be another coal man and the little Candelaria Square will have another steeple and other bells. But the sea will always be there! The sea! And the flames will always be there, licking at Ana Isabel's feet who's gone to hell because she committed a sacrilege. Ana Isabel gulps down the cup of coffee in one swallow and grabs old Estefanía who can barely follow her and struggles to keep up with her. Ana Isabel runs down the cobblestone streets, stops suddenly, and starts running again. It's a cold morning. A dazzling December morning. They are selling oranges on the corner of Santa Barbara at two cents apiece and some children are eating them and throwing away the rinds that shine defiantly on the cobblestones. Ana Isabel is about to receive her First Communion. It's not going to be a part of a Solemn Ceremony, she won't be wearing a long veil, or the rose wreath. Her mother altered the white dress, the one with the pleats. She's already put on a new collar and will buy the ribbon. She'll receive her Solemn Communion next year. Her mother promised her. Since, according to the teacher, you can receive your First Communion twice... Maybe it's because girls like her will be able to wear a veil over their foreheads and the wreath and look pretty, even if it's just for once. The poor, ugly girls like Ana Isabel. Why should she be ugly? She has big eyes. But their color is so light! And she is so thin and pale. Why can't she be like her brother? Her brother is so handsome. When they are out together everyone stops them in the street and people ask:

"Whose boy is that? What a handsome child!"

Ana Isabel stands up straight and moves over in hope that someone will say that about her.

"What a handsome boy! God bless him!"

And Ana Isabel's eyes cloud up. Why can't she be like her brother? But that's also a sin, wanting to be as good-looking as her brother. The teacher said that's called envy and it's the worst of sins. Ana Isabel thinks about sin. This is a sin, that's a sin, everything's a sin. And at confession she'll have to tell all her sins to Padre Mayorca if she wants to receive her First Communion. The monotonous rain keeps falling. The classroom fills with the smell of wet earth and flowers stripped of their petals. The teacher runs her fingers through her rosary, a rosary of large black beads. The girls kneel and cross themselves and the classroom fills with childish voices.

"Holy Mary, Mother of God..."

"Ora pro nobis, ora pro nobis..."

The teacher recites the litany.

"Queen of Angels, Star of the Morning."

The Star of the morning must be that little star, almost blue, Ana Isabel has seen early, twinkling between the gray clouds.

"Tower of Ivory..."

Of Ivory! Like elephant tusks. But it won't have a bell. It will have one thousand little windows, it will be like climbing towards the heavens and when the sun hides, it will turn rosy, like the poppies.

"Ora pro nobis, ora pro nobis..."

The teacher opens the window. It's stopped raining and only the drops of water in the Royal Palm shake themselves loose and fall to the ground. The earth goes "glug" as it sucks in the thick drops. Ana Isabel would love to take off her shoes and run barefoot over the wet earth. Ana Isabel loves the sun, but she also loves the rain, and when it rains, she has a crazy impulse to go barefoot, without clothes, and run naked in the rain. When Aunt Clara heard this, she commented severely that Ana Isabel has the instincts of a wicked woman, a woman of the streets. A woman of the streets? That must be Trinidad, the one who sells bread, or Domitila who sells arepas. But Ana Isabel has never seen Trinidad or Domitila run naked in the rain. And Aunt Clara has said this is a sin, a sin against modesty, a shameful sin...

34

"You must not love your body," Aunt Clara is always repeating. "The body is the soul's punishment." But Ana Isabel loves her body. She loves the arms that she lifts very high, the legs she runs with, the eyes she sees with... And Ana Isabel loves her hands. In the afternoon when night approaches and she's looking at the stars from the patio, by herself, all alone, she kisses her hands. That is how the prince will do it, the prince who is waiting for Ana Isabel...

"It stopped raining," the teacher says. "Get ready to go to confession. To examine your conscience."

The girls look up their sins in a little dark hard-covered book. Every time she reads this book Ana Isabel feels bad, with so many sins she's afraid she can't remember them all. In this book the sins are listed but Ana Isabel doesn't know what they mean. "Don't fornicate." Ana Isabel had asked the teacher, who kept quiet and then said it's a sin little girls can't commit. But Ana Isabel has committed many sins. The sin of envy, because she wants to be pretty. The sin of gluttony because she likes the food when she goes to piñata parties. She devours the white meringues and the shiny candies. The teacher says that Ana Isabel's nature is prone to sensual. A sensual nature, and who knows where that will take her. Sensual. Ana Isabel looked it up in the dictionary. "Sensual: an excessive inclination towards the pleasure of the senses."

There are five senses, sight, smell, hearing, tasting, and touching. Of course she's sensual. She likes to see, see it all and hear and taste, even when it's the sin of gluttony. And to smell? The scent of magnolias and lilies makes her dizzy. And she senses the perfume flowing through her body, now it's in her mouth, now in her eyes, now in her hands... Without a doubt she'll have to tell Father Mayorca that she's sensual. Of having sinful thoughts. Of loving her body, which is the soul's punishment. And also what her cousin Luis told her. She'll have to tell it all, all, because Ana Isabel doesn't want eternal damnation. After the rain, the sun came out. A yellow sun, a bright golden sun that sees itself reflected in the wet streets. The streets where girls walk by two by two, in their white capes and their dark hard-covered books. The church has a stained glass window in which a very blond Jesus is preaching in front of blue mountains. Inside the confessional Father Mayorca awaits. The girls are pushing each other; no one wants to be the first. Luisa Figueroa approaches saying that she's not afraid of making her confession because she's done it other times and she's always gotten a small penance, proof that she has no sins. The teacher orders them to be quiet. The girls cross their arms and kneel down in a row.

Ana Isabel is fifth in line. Fifth. After Luisa Figueroa who is kneeling next to the confessional comes Esperanza Caldera, then Justina, then Cecilia and then...Ana Isabel.

"Dear God! Dear God! Make me good, for I am bad. Dear God! Make me good!" Ana Isabel presses her hands that are crossed together against her chest.

"Make me good, for I am bad!"

On the high altar the candles flicker in front of the Virgin of Sorrows. The Virgin who is Goodness itself.

How can the Virgin always be so good?

"Dear God! Make me good, make me good!"

Out on the street the lottery salesman calls out, "The big ticket! I have four left. Lucky Eight! I've got it!" The voice echoes from afar, there under the wide vault near the flickering candles.

"Now it's your turn..."

It's Cecilia talking. Cecilia is pale and she wears a forced smile.

"Go ahead, Ana Isabel, now it's your turn..."

Ana Isabel doesn't know how she made it to the confessional, or how she knelt without falling down.

Confession

"Recite the Act of Contrition, my daughter..."

Ana Isabel's trembling little face lies next to the grid with the metallic smell, like her father's breath. But it's Father Mayorca's breath that falls on Ana Isabel's face, who throws her head back because it makes her a little nauseous.

"Go ahead, my little daughter, recite the Act of Contrition."

"I, a sinner confess to God... And...who will come to judge the living and the dead... No, no, I a sinner, confess to God..."

No matter how hard she tries, Ana Isabel can't remember what comes next. And if she can't recite the Act of Contrition, her sins won't be forgiven.

"I confess to God..."

"Tell me your sins, my child..."

"Father, it's that... I..."

"Go on, tell me your sins because it's already late and there are many more. Come on, I will help you..."

And Father Mayorca interrogates Ana Isabel. He asks her a lot of things and to all of them Ana Isabel replies in the affirmative because she's committed all the sins Father Mayorca asked her about. But ah, no, Ana Isabel doesn't understand what Father Mayorca is asking her now...

"Come, child, don't be ashamed to confess it. You must say it so it can be forgiven and washed away with the waters of the blessed sacrament of confession... Go on, child, make a small effort"

The candles continue to flicker. In the street the vendor shouts "Lucky Eight!" Behind the grid Father Mayorca pronounces every syllable. As he exhales, his breath falls thickly on Ana Isabel's face.

"Go on, my child, don't be ashamed, God is merciful to sinners..."

Sacrilege! Eternity! Eternity forever! With her hands clasped tightly together, held close against her breast, Ana Isabel cries.

The Silver Tray

*I*t's the day of the retreat. Ana Isabel has to stay at the school just like all the other girls who are going to receive their First Communion. Here come the trays full of food. Ana Isabel looks toward the patio, toward the gate of the entryway, waiting for Estefanía. Cecilia is going to eat in the same room with the children, with Justina and Esmeralda Caldera. Luisa Figueroa alone, on the teacher's round table. Her lunch has already arrived. A large tray the gardener brought, because Luisa is rich and she lives in the neighborhood of El Paraíso in a big house with a big garden. Ana Isabel and Jaime saw it on Sundays, when they went on a ride on a tram through El Paraíso. Ana Isabel steals glances to see what they brought for Luisa Figueroa. Chicken! Luisa Figueroa is going to eat chicken! And grapes! Green, crystal-clear grapes. And a big glass of milk. What's that thing on the little tray? Something with cream... Oh, it must be delicious! And the napkins! White and embroidered... Esmeralda Caldera and Cecilia also have a delicious lunch of chicken, fruit, sweets... So she can't eat with anyone else because surely they'll bring what they eat at her house: rice, beans... She'll eat all alone. She'll go to the grownup's room which is deserted and no one will see her and make fun of her...

"Ana Isabel, hasn't your lunch arrived yet? Come with us, we're waiting for you."

It's Cecilia calling her. Cecilia likes Ana Isabel a lot, and she also likes Cecilia. One day, Cecilia was crying because her little bird died and Ana Isabel hugged her close, Cecilia, who hid her face and wouldn't let anyone even look at her...

The Silver Tray

At last, Estefanía arrived with the lunch! They sent it on a silver tray. It's part of the coffee service they hardly ever use and is locked up in the display cabinet in the dining room. It's the silver service Ana Isabel and Jaime often admire. A wedding present from Uncle Marcelino, her father's uncle. Ana Isabel and Jaime hardly ever see Uncle Marcelino. Just once a year, at Christmas. It's a big day for them. They are dressed in their best clothes. Ana Isabel can only think about the present Uncle Marcelino will give them. Uncle Marcelino is a dried out little old man who wears a silk cap and leather slippers. He has a lot of money. Her father says he owns a coffee plantation and another one of cacao, so big, that it takes days and days to travel through it. But Uncle Marcelino is not nice. He's never said a kind word.

"Ana Isabel, say hello to Uncle Marcelino."

Ana Isabel stays close to the doorway. Ana Isabel doesn't like the room where Uncle Marcelino receives them. The walls are covered with portraits painted in oil in big gilded frames. Portraits of the Alcántaras. And they all have a cold, hard air about them within their frames. It's a closed-off room. It doesn't have any windows and you can't see out to the patio or catch a glimpse of the sky. It smells like mothballs, worm-eaten silk and Uncle Marcelino sitting stiffly on an armchair that is upholstered in damask. The other furnishings are covered with white rough linen, but Ana Isabel knows that they are red, like the armchair, because on the day of the tree, they are removed and everyone can sit on the damask. Uncle Marcelino doesn't have any children, or a wife, because he's not married. What does he need so much money? Her father says he spent a lot of money travelling. He's lived in Paris for a long time and he speaks French. The Izaguirre cousins call him "grand oncle" but Ana Isabel and Jaime simply call him Uncle Marcelino. Uncle Marcelino doesn't like Venezuela and neither do the Izaguirres. Mrs. Izaguirre longs to live in Paris. The Champs Elysées! Au Bon Marché! Au Bon Marché! That big store that has so many floors and even an elevator. That's where they buy the blue wool suits with the white collars that Josefina and Luis wear... The silver tray has a monogram in the middle: AK. Alcántara, Krauss. Krauss with a K, because Ana Isabel's grandfather was German.

Grandfather also wore a cap like Uncle Marcelino, but he didn't look like him at all. Grandfather Krauss loved Ana Isabel and Jaime a lot. On rainy days he would sit with them by the window and he would make them little paper boats. The dark, dirty water ran down the cobblestone streets. The little boat would fold its wet sails and almost capsize among the dirty paper and broken alpargatas the current washed down from the hills... "There go Captain Jaime and the schooner 'Ana Isabel' sailing down the Rhine..." And Grandfather, with his blue eyes and his blond mustache would laugh. The Rhine was the only thing Grandfather remembered about Germany. The Rhine with its gay and turbulent waters. Because he had been born in Venezuela and it was there where he worked the land. Ana Isabel listened in astonishment when Grandfather spoke about the hacienda, where it was cold and the trees were so tall... How he rose early at dawn and drank his coffee with the workers, eating hard square biscuits and hard white cheese. Because of what he ate Grandfather was more creole than any mulatto, more so than any black man from Barlovento. He liked beans, meat fried with onions and tomatoes and hallacas and coffee with dark brown sugar. On the plantation he sang Venezuelan songs with a soft well-tempered voice, accompanying himself on the guitar. Those were the good old days. Grandfather Krauss was a sturdy and happy man. In the plantation's room he swayed in the hammock surrounded by his family and his workers.

The Silver Tray

At night he taught his children. It was a night school. After dinner, which was served at six, Grandfather would get out his pencils and his notebooks and classes would begin. History, Geometry, Arithmetic, even French and dancing... Tra la la, Tra, la la, Two steps to the right, two turns to the left! Grandfather Krauss sang "Over the Waves" or "Goodbye to Ocumare." Sometimes, remembering his father, he intoned very romantic *lieds* that he mixed up with songs from the plains. But the good old days were over soon. The old Venezuelan political wrongs returned and Grandfather was exiled to Curaçao and he lost all his land. Whenever Grandfather reminisced about his exile for Ana Isabel, his eyes clouded over and he spoke of the island with a dull voice. Of the starry skies and the warm nights on "La Otra Banda." Of the calm waters where you could see white sailboats and little black children who dived for a shilling the tourists from across the Atlantic threw to them. There, too, like before, his forgotten teaching skills resurfaced and he taught once again. But then it was the children of the exiled in Curacao who recited from the primer and the history of Frederick the Great. During siesta time on the island it seemed like life came to a standstill. When work slowed down and the sluggish bodies that were bathed in sweat stopped in their last efforts, Don Juan Krauss earned a few shillings tuning pianos. His blue eyes smiled sadly as he leaned to the sound of the strings. Then, Grandfather's hands would run across the keys of the out-of-tune pianos on that black island heavy with the tropics while the chords of the romantic *lieds* and *corridos* floated up...

But grandfather had died.

Grandfather died when Ana Isabel had just turned six. That day she saw him stretched out on the bed with his hands folded and a white handkerchief covering his face. Why the white handkerchief? Why the folded hands? Grandfather's hands wouldn't be making paper boats any

41

more. On rainy days when the stream from the hills brought down dirty papers and broken alpargatas "Captain Jaime" and the schooner "Ana Isabel" wouldn't sail down the Rhine with their swollen sails. After seeing her grandfather laid out on the bed, Ana Isabel was gripped by a terrible fear of death. At night, folding her hands across her chest the same as her Grandfather and closing her eyes, she would say to herself, "I am dead!" Then she would start shaking and yelling loudly, so loudly that Mrs. Alcántara, hearing the screams, would hurry to Ana Isabel's side and try to calm Ana Isabel who repeated,

"I'm dead! I'm dead!"

Why does she have to die? Ana Isabel knows that birds die, the baker's donkey died and he had to hitch another donkey to the bread wagon. Dogs die. Justina's dog Bob died. They buried him in the yard under the soursop tree... Ants die. Ana Isabel kills them, that is to say, she used to kill them and now she doesn't do it anymore once she found out that being dead means being still forever. There are many ants in the patio of her house. Ana Isabel, lying on the floor, observes them for hours. Ants file by laden down with green blades of grass and little pieces of earth. At times, their load is so heavy and the ants are so small that's it's too much for them and Ana Isabel helps them along. When she crosses the patio she isn't as careless as she was before, when she didn't know what death was. Now, she crosses it slowly, looking down on the ground so she doesn't step on the ants... Animals die, and also people. Grandfather died. And her mother, she'll have to die and her father and her little brother Jaime and herself, Ana Isabel, she'll have to die... And after she's dead, what will Ana Isabel do? Where will she go? They put Grandfather in a black box and later welded it shut. Ana Isabel listened for a long time to the buzzing of the Primus that sounded like a motor, like the locomotives of the trains Ana Isabel likes so much. But Ana Isabel doesn't like the sound of the Primus. She ran to the yard so as not to hear it but she still heard it from afar, monotonous, and she had to put her hands over her ears like she did when she was afraid. Now in the yard Ana Isabel forgot that they were welding the box Grandfather was in and she would never see him again. The yard was silent. Estefanía and Gregoria were in Grandfather's room with Jaime, looking at the wreaths. The yard was deserted and it seemed larger. It was almost noon. The sun had suddenly hidden itself. Ana Isabel, flung down on the ground, under the guasimo tree's canopy was chewing on a black slimy fruit and suddenly started to cry out loud, with loud sobs, with her face flat on the ground. Crying for her grandfather, for her mother, for her father, for her little brother Jaime, and for herself, for Ana Isabel, crying for everyone that has to die...

The silver tray is big and heavy and Estefanía grumbles because Ana Isabel wants to carry it by herself. "Look child, don't come jumping around me or I'll drop the tray."

Finally, between the two of them, they brought it to the grownup's room. The room is empty. Ana Isabel sets the tray on the table next to the rulers and the inkwells. Oh, but what have they sent her? She also has sweets, peach sweets. And an omelet. And potatoes. Can it be a holiday at her house today? But it's not her mother's or her father's saint's day. It's December, and it's no one in her family's saint's day. So, then, what's the holiday? Did they all of a sudden come into money? Did they get rich while she was away at the retreat? Estefanía is waiting in the hallway. Ana Isabel is dying to ask her. Had they become rich? They'd gotten rich! So that her mother doesn't have to work and she can buy dresses like her mother's friends and they'll give Jaime and her bicycles and skates like Cecilia's. The teacher is eating her lunch. She could tiptoe to the hallway where Estefanía is, without anyone seeing her. Old

Estefanía is sitting by the doorway that leads to the hall. She is singing softly, is Old Estefanía:

How dark is the night
And shadowy the path...
Oh, my love!
And shadowy the path...

She sings sadly as she keeps time on the cement floor with her hand:

But since I love you
I always find a way...
Oh, my love!
I always find a way...

If they've suddenly gotten rich, Estefanía doesn't look happy about it. Estefanía always sings when she's sad. Up until the day her grandfather died Ana Isabel heard her singing so softly that she had to guess what she was singing.

But...what about that lunch?

"Estefanía, where did they find the money?" Ana Isabel is frightened by the sound of her own voice in the silent hall.

"The money? Go on child, what money are they going to find? No money. What money is there going to be?"

"And...the lunch?"

"What about the lunch? The lunch is for you alone. Your mother fried you up that omelet and bought a half a kilo of peaches for you. The lunch is for you alone. Go on, girl, can't you see you're on a retreat?"

Ana Isabel doesn't ask any more questions. Walking slowly, she goes back to the room. Estefanía sits near the gate in the entrance:

How dark is the night
And shadowy the path...
Oh, my love!
And shadowy the path...

Ana Isabel's lunch is on the table, on the silver tray.

The Silver Tray

The omelet, the peach treat on the little round crystal dish. All is clean and carefully laid out, covered with a very clean white napkin. But Ana Isabel isn't hungry. Her mouth is dry and there is a lump in her throat. She feels like crying. But what is Ana Isabel crying about? She sits down and cuts off a piece of the omelet and starts chewing it. Her eyes cloud up as though she is about to cry. But, why shouldn't Ana Isabel cry? The sound of scraping chairs comes from the teacher's room. In the little girls' classroom Justina's fresh laughter and Esperanza Caldera's shrill voice can be heard.

"Hey, don't laugh so loudly, it's a sin."

A Voice Sings from Afar

Ana Isabel has received her First Communion. She marched down the central nave of the church while Carmen Otaño's solemn and peaceful voice sang in the choir.

"Here my Lord, so great and so desired, offers himself to me for the first time..."

The altar boy, whose name is not Pepe, but Roberto, is short and fat and fourteen years old and has raised the censer several times and the girls float by enveloped in the palpable magic of the smoke. The incense's fragrance envelops Ana Isabel, who feels happy and sad at the same time, a sweet sadness that makes her sigh. Now she doesn't feel like jumping, running, lying down on the damp grass, bathing in the river, or climbing to the top of the mango tree... She would like to stay there, enveloped in the blue smoke, wanting not to be... To be smoke, flame, fragrance...

Ana Isabel already received her First Communion... Our Lord's body tasted like bread, toasted bread, and Ana Isabel is afraid because Our Lord's body between her lips tasted like toasted bread... But the songs, the incense and the bells make her feel light-headed. "He offers himself to me, he offers himself to me for the first time..."

Carmen Otaño's voice calms and lulls... The serene singing voice, the girls dressed in white, holding slender candles in their hands... And her longing to stay there forever. Wanting not to be herself. To be smoke, flame, fragrance...

Ana Isabel has received her First Communion. Nothing has changed.

A Voice Sings from Afar

In the square, the trees reach out their branches like always, sheltering the children who play in their shade. During the months of the dry season the earth is parched and grass hardly grows. Dry leaves invade the square and the wind gathers them near the roots of the ceiba tree. Clouds of dust escape from the earth and redden the children's eyes as they look up towards the tops of the maría trees. When it rains, the grass turns green and grows tall. That's when they can play "The Moors." They sit in a row, holding hands in the newly-grown grass.

The Moors are coming!

Here they come!

The Moors are coming!

What should we do?

Fall down dead!

Lying on the grass with their heads close together, they mingle their breath and their stifled laughter. Up high in the clear sky the swallows fly by swiftly. Some of them perch between the trolley lines. Nothing has changed.

The days flow by, months. The month of Ana Isabel's First Communion Day is far behind.

Better times await. Do they? Ana Isabel is the one who's waiting, since Mrs. Alcántara doesn't tire of repeating that life will always be like this. Mrs. Alcántara is always sad. She says, "This country" and "this life" with a conclusive tone of desperation. Ana Isabel thinks there must be other countries and other lives where mothers aren't sad and don't spend their days making cigarette boxes and sewing soldier's uniforms.

The cigarette boxes entertain Ana Isabel when it's raining and she and Jaime can't go outside to play. They feel all grown-up helping their mother. The boxes are white with red letters. "La Favorita Cigarettes." The glue is in an empty butter tin. You put glue on the paper and then fold it over a block of wood and you slam it against the table. At first, Ana Isabel enjoyed making boxes. It was like learning a new game.

"Careful you put the letters on straight, Ana Isabel! You put those on backwards."

"Pay attention, my child! First you glue the front, then the back, and the tips of the sides. You see, like this!"

Ana Isabel had fun! She even bet Jaime who could make the most boxes. But there are also sunny days with clear skies. Ana Isabel wants to play in the square, but she has to help her mother. She sits at the dining room table, at her mother's side, facing Jaime. Dusk falls slowly. The last rays of the sun, a red sun that filters through the blinds, shines on Mrs. Alcántara's tired face. Jaime wants Ana Isabel to tell him a story when they are done. Ana Isabel is proud that her brother always wants her to tell him stories. When she's older she is going to write big, thick books like Salgari's.

How many boxes left to make?

Two hundred more.

Two hundred!

"La Favorita Cigarettes! The Favorite Cigarettes!"

Ana Isabel thinks about the sultan who has a favorite. A sultan who wears a turban and loose trousers.

"When we are done, I'll tell you the story about the sultan who had a favorite. A sultan who wears a turban and loose trousers. When we're done I'll tell you the story about 'The Favorite.'"

"The Favorite like the cigarette boxes?"

"Don't be silly. The boxes are ugly and sad, and this is a nice, happy story."

Of course the boxes are ugly and sad. None of her friends has to stop going to the square to play to make boxes instead. Her friends' mothers don't have to work. Ana Isabel always finds them in the hallway, reading or doing embroidery when she goes looking for her friends, or she finds them in the foyer, all dressed up, ready to go visit other children. None of her friends has to stop playing in the square and work making little cigarette boxes, not even Otilia, the little olive-skinned girl who lives on the other side of the square and whom her mother tells her it's not a good idea to play with because she's not respectable. Respectable people. Is disreputable the opposite of respectable? Is Otilia disreputable? Why is it always the poor who are not respectable? But Ana Isabel isn't rich. At least her mother never stops telling her that she's poor, but respectable nevertheless. Ana Isabel is confused. Gregoria, whom she asked about it one day replied:

"Look, girl, there's only the rich and the poor. The rich enjoy, the poor endure..."

Mrs. Alcántara has turned on the light, because she can't see any more. They all sit quietly. You can only hear the "clunk, clunk" the little boxes make as they fall into the basket which is almost full. From far away, maybe it's coming from Otilia's house, a voice is singing. It sings sweetly, dragging out the syllables.

"He offers himself to me, he offers himself to me for the first time..."

The voice is carried by the wind. It carries across the square, floats through the ceiba tree, above the tops of the maría trees and the tall branches of the possumwood.

It comes from afar. Perhaps from Otilia's house. Perhaps from down the street where the children are stretched out on the ground playing marbles. The wind carries the voice, brings it, takes it far away. It will get lost. But no, here it is, close by, close to Ana Isabel, almost next to her.

The voice sings :

"Here is my Lord, so great, so desired..."

It sings and evokes memories of girls in white dresses enveloped in blue smoke.

49

The voice sings.

It rises up to the reddened sky and falls from above in dark notes, hovering over the earth. Ana Isabel listens with a vacant expression holding the cigarette box in her hands.

"He offers himself to me, he offers himself to me, for the first time."

"Jaime, do you remember the day I received my First Communion?"

The Field Trip

pril. May, June, July...July is exam month. The girls are studying hard. At night Ana Isabel's eyes close and she sees only numbers, fractions, divisions...

"Hurry up, Ana Isabel, so you can get twenty points and you can go on the field trip."

Ana Isabel can't think of anything else except the field trip. Last year she almost lost the chance to go. She still remembers how scared she was.

"What?" Mrs. Alcántara had asked. "Six kilos of meat? But that teacher must be out of her mind. How am I going to get enough to buy six kilos of meat? If that's the case, you're not going on the field trip."

The teacher wasn't out of her mind. Esperanza Caldera and Luisa Figueroa were put in charge of bringing the meat. Ana Isabel and Cecilia Guillén would bring bread.

"Well, bread...that's another thing. We'll have Nemesio bring us three large loaves, the kind that cost a bolívar each..."

Ana Isabel couldn't sleep the night before.

"But child, look how you toss and turn in that bed! If that's what you're going to do, I won't let you go on the field trip..."

She'd gotten up before dawn. The house was silent. Everyone else was asleep. A fading moon was balancing on the trolley wire overhead. It was cold. It was still night. On the trees, the shadows fall between the still leaves. Daylight was still far away. Only a light and golden glow came slowly down from the hills to announce its presence.

"But what are you doing up, Ana Isabel! It's the middle of the night, my child! Go back to bed and lie still there until I tell you. What a child, dear Lord!"

51

Ana Isabel had quietly gone back to bed. With half-opened eyes, she waited for morning.

"At least have a cup of coffee and milk. You're going to faint along the way. For goodness' sake, I've never seen anyone so worked up over a field trip!"

Estefanía was shivering from the cold.

"Lordy, you be up early, girl!"

"I'm going on a field trip. An fi-eld tr-ip..."

"Girl, you gonna make me fall. Leave me be. Missus, call Ana Isabel to come inside..."

Chucuto was lying beside the door.

"I'm going to 'The Falls,' Chucuto, I'm going..."

From the window Jaime followed her with sad eyes.

"You'll also get to go on field trips, child. Don't make that face!"

"Good bye, Chucuto! Good bye, Jaime! Good bye little square. I'm leaving. I'm leaving and I'm not coming back. Good bye! Good bye!"

"Wait up, girl, don't run so fast!"

Ana Isabel arrived at the school panting. The teacher hadn't gotten up yet. In the patio the leaves were heavy with dew and Ana Isabel was shaking them one by one so she could watch the drops tremble and fall as they shone from the sun.

"I have the meat."

"And I have bread..."

"Me, the salad..."

"And the jelly and cheese?"

"The jelly, Justina. And the cheese?"

"Be quiet, girls. The truck's not here yet."

José del Carmen, the driver, was a good-looking black man with bulging eyes. When his face appeared between the fence, the girls burst out laughing and started to run away.

"Hmm, that's not OK by me. If that's how it's gonna be, I'm not taking you..."

The Field Trip

But José del Carmen made friends with all of them. He put a chair in the middle of the truck bed for the teacher to sit on. The girls would have to stand up. The floor was littered with parcels full of bathing suits, dishes, glasses, trays of food... The truck bumped along the dusty road lifting up startled flocks of wrens.

"Now we're coming to Chacao. We've already passed by Sabana Grande."

"And what about that big house, what is it, José del Carmen?"

"You see, that one they call La Floresta."

"We already went past El Muñeco."

"El Muñeco? The Doll? What doll, Jose del Carmen?"

The air was bright. The sun began warming it up.

"Put your hats on, girls. You're going to catch cold."

The truck was traveling through coffee plantations scraping the hedges of flowering sage and blooming lutea.

"Faster, José del Carmen, faster!"

"Oh, yeah? You want us to turn over?"

"Look at the butterflies! A yellow one. Another one the color of fire. And the dragonfly."

"A visitor's coming. A visitor's coming."

"We're arriving at Los Dos Caminos."

"Now we are going past the Hacienda 'San José'..."

"What a big hacienda, José del Carmen!"

The coral trees were in bloom. They spread their slender boughs above the coffee plants. The coffee was ripening. Big iridescent flies were beating their wings. The ground was carpeted with soft red petals. The truck climbed noisily, heading uphill towards the falls. The girls were singing and their pure voices floated above the bright, warm July morning.

I had a doll with a blue dress...

With a low-cut collar and in the camisole...

"Good. Here's where the river brought us! This is it, we can't go any farther."

The motor breathed energetically. José del Carmen wiped his sweat off with the back of his hand. "Ah! We're here already? That was fast..."

"Careful, girls. Come down slowly."

"See you this afternoon, José del Carmen. Be here at five, alright?"

"At five? That's too early. At six, Miss, at six!..."

"No, sir. I'm not going on that dark road to get to Caracas at night. At five on the dot, you know that, José del Carmen. At five..."

"Good bye, José del Carmen! See you at six! Until six o'clock..."

"Let's get going, it's getting late. Team up with a partner. Walk two-by-two."

Ana Isabel was walking with Cecilia. It was a narrow path. On one side was the mountain and on the other side the river flowed gently. The path was shaded by huge mango trees. Water lapped up gently between the rocks where ferns grew.

"Look at the bocado mango tree!"

"And the one with the big hilacha!"

"This one's ripe, Ana Isabel!"

"There's a spotted one. Let's take it down."

"Girls, don't throw rocks. Don't stop so often or we'll never get there."

"Look at the ferns, Miss. On the way back we'll pick them. There's a fishtail fern, a maidenhair fern, bridal wreath..."

"Keep walking girls, keep walking..."

The teacher walked from side to side keeping an eye on them. She wore a cane leaf hat pulled down to her eyebrows. Her eyes shone more than usual and from time to time you could hear her coughing.

Ana Isabel straggled behind gathering branches of blue poinsettia.

The Field Trip

"Make way, here comes a donkey."

The path was so narrow that the donkey's flanks brushed against the girls' bare arms. It's a bell-ringer. "Where did you leave the rest of the team?"

The herdsman with his trousers rolled half-way up his legs walked behind holding a stick.

"Don't hit it, man. Don't be a brute!"

"Girls, you leave that man alone or he might say something rude."

The herdsman looked at the girls wordlessly with his slanted, colorless eyes.

The sweet scent of cowpats, hierba brava and malojillo could be smelled along the way. The purple herons sang up high in the mango tree. Among the loud crickets and bittersweet and the cujíyou could hear the cooing of a dove,

"Listen! A Turkish dove."

"Could she be in her nest? Let's find her!"

"It's a tinamou, listen to her song."

"Girls, don't fall behind. Ana Isabel Alcántara!" the teacher called out in a strict voice.

A dirty barefoot woman was coming down the bank. She balanced a bucket of clean, wrung- out laundry on her head. Two naked little children eating mangos were clinging to her skirts.

"How's the river, ma'am?"

The woman smiled pleasantly at the girls.

"Has it risen?"

"Just a bit, just a tiny bit, not more than that."

"Is the pool very deep? I'd be afraid!"

"Miss, we're going to bathe at La Batea, The Washpan."

"No, sir. I'm not crazy enough to go with you to La Batea. We're going to Ño Alejandro, as you well know, to Ño Alejandro. Keep walking, keep walking, we're just about there."

The river had barely risen. A light golden glow shimmered on the surface of the pool. Wide and good-natured, Ño Alejandro opened up, dressed in foam and decked with yellow flowers and savanna guava trees.

"Be careful, girls. Be careful as you change; there's lots of trash here."

The teacher started taking off her clothes behind a rock. The girls were lying down on the grass trying to catch a glimpse of her off-guard as she undressed. But the teacher was crouching, covering herself with her dress so you could only see her shoulder from where her high-necked blouse was sliding down.

"Did you see her?"

"I couldn't. And you?"

"Me neither."

Ana Isabel was undressing next to Cecilia. She took off her dress showing off the ribbons with blue embroidery that her mother had sewn on the hem of her petticoat.

"How pretty!" Cecilia said.

"All my underwear is like that," Ana Isabel lied shamelessly.

"Ooh, the water is so cold!"

"Don't be silly, jump in."

"Jump in, it's not deep."

When Ana Isabel got into the pool the teacher had already reached the falls. Her hair was loose, black and shiny. A brilliant head of hair that fell below her waist. Her low-cut undershirt showed off her very white arms, her round shoulders, her slender neck. Foam was running around all over her, reaching up to her lips, bouncing off her hair... She seemed like another person. She laughed as she leapt and threw her head back. Air entered her blouse and inflated it so it looked like a red balloon floating above the water. The girls pressed their hands against it. Tiny little bubbles that looked like soapsuds stood still for a moment, and then they were swept away by the current as they burst, tinted with color, alive with light, leaving barely a shadow of foam.

Ana Isabel didn't recognize the teacher. The milky white arms crisscrossed with blue veins. And what lovely hair!...

Ana Isabel watched it as it went under water and then came up once more to the surface like living roots, dark wet roots that smelled of the jungle, like turbid risen water. Could it be that that teacher was pretty? Ana Isabel had never thought about that. At school she only heard her voice, a bit muted and dull. About her hands that held chalk, book, ruler. Always wearing a high-necked, long-sleeved blouse. She had never looked at her eyes, she'd never heard her laugh... Could it be that the teacher was pretty? At the bottom of the pool you could grab sand by the handful. Tiny little silver sardines swam quickly by and hid themselves among the rocks. You could hardly see the path where the herdsman was whipping the team shouting,

"Oy, soo, oy, soo!"

Could it be that the teacher was pretty?

In the afternoon, heading back, Ana Isabel still asked herself that. The teacher had gone back to being who she always was. With her long-sleeved blouse with the high collar hiding the very white arms. Her beautiful hair gathered up in a big bun on her neck, the straw hat pulled down to her eyebrows.

The truck made its way slowly through the dark road. The teacher sat stiffly in the chair with her hands folded over her skirt and said not a word. José del Carmen was smoking and the bright red tip of his cigarette broke through the starless night. Ana Isabel leaned against the side and watched the road, now a white smudge that opened up ahead. The night-blooming jasmine's fragrance filled the air. The fireflies shone in the night. The crickets sang in the coffee plants. Could it be that the teacher was pretty?

The Deer

Where's the deer coming from?
From the burning hill.
What's it got in its scorched tail?
Let's run and go see...

Hands clasp. White hands, dark hands, with stained fingers and nails cut down to the quick. Little girls' hands. A weak sun shines into the school's patio and La Negra Nicasia sweeps the yard. La Negra Nicasia does all the housework. She sweeps, cleans, cooks and washes and irons clothes. Her cotton petticoat is gathered up and she's barefoot.

"No girls, go somewhere else with your songs. It's me who has to pay if the clothes aren't white enough..."

But in the upstairs patio you can't play "The Deer." It has a dirt floor with a very tall Royal Palm and the teacher's roses and jasmines and heliotropes are there.

And in the hallway they're playing "The Serpent."

The serpent, the serpent of the sea...
This way you may come...
This way I will pass...
And one girl will be left behind...

"The teacher said we could play here..."

"Well, I don't know about that. They better not come telling me the clothes got dirty."

Ana Isabel likes La Negra Nicasia a lot. She always lets her have whatever brown sugar is in the sugar bowl. Because it's brown sugar and not white sugar in the sugar bowl. The teacher is very poor and brown sugar costs less.

The Deer

The sugar bowl is full of ground brown sugar, a light-colored brown sugar that looks like honey. Ana Isabel fills her mouth with it and imagines she's eating honey. Honey from bees.

Perucho goes past her house with his basket full of honeycombs.

"Bee honey for good girls! Bee honey makes you blush and cures colds. I have bee honey."

Ana Isabel never buys honey. How could she with only two cents for a snack?

She buys a tamarind bar and second-rate chocolate. First-rate chocolate costs more and comes wrapped in silver paper. Esperanza Caldera and Luisa Figueroa always eat high quality chocolate and they save the silver wrappers to send to the missionaries to help them save the Chinese, who don't know about God, nor do they know about heaven, hell and purgatory. The missionaries will teach them all about it and also about sin. Ana Isabel didn't know what sin was. Father Mayorca taught her about it and since then Ana Isabel sins a lot. Ana Isabel knows about the Chinese. The Chinese wash and iron. They do nothing but wash and iron. On the way to school there's a Chinese laundry. The windows are always open. Ana Isabel climbed onto the bars and stayed to watch the Chinese press the iron firmly over the damp shirts. Chinamen are yellow. There are four races. At least that's what the geography book Ana Isabel is studying says. White, red, black and yellow. Why isn't everyone the same? Ana Isabel is white. The Chinese are yellow. Nicasia and Estefanía are black and so is Eusebio, the son of the clerk at the grocery store "The Chimborazo." In Venezuela there are many blacks. Blacks are not respectable. She is not allowed to be with black people. But there are also white people she isn't allowed to play with.

"Those folks, you can't tell where they're from," says Mrs. Alcántara.

Perico and Carmencita and Pepe the altar boy aren't black, but it's almost as if they were, because her mother won't let her play with them. Luisa Figueroa is dark, very dark, almost black! Ana Isabel thinks, but she's rich and she lives in El Paraíso, and only respectable people live there. Whenever Ana Isabel meets a new girl Mrs. Alcántara asks her who her parents are. Ana Isabel never remembers and has to ask them again.

"Oh, Tula Madriz's daughter! By the way, Tula made a bad marriage, with some unknown boy from the interior... What's her father's name? What? Sinforoso Alfonso? Now there are some strange people. It's so hard to meet good people these days. This is Pepe Pancho's niece. Look, Federico! Pepe Pancho's grandaughter. Of course I know who she is. Ask your mother if she remembers the Krausses from Altagracia. How about that! Pepe's grandaughter!"

But Ana Isabel likes to play with Perico and Carmencita, with Pepe the altar boy and little black Eusebio. Little black Eusebio knows an endless number of games and songs. He sings to verses he composes. He says they come from his noggin and Eusebio raises his hands to his wooly head and laughs with teeth so white they are Ana Isabel's envy. Little black Eusebio is better at playing "The Deer" than Justina, than Cecilia and also better than Luisa Figueroa. He always comes up with new verses for the deer and when it's time to form a chain little black Eusebio's is stronger than anyone's.

"It's made of iron," he says smiling.

Eusebio's arm is made of iron and as hard as all of them try, it's impossible to break through. Ana Isabel looks at her thin hand in Eusebio's thick black one and is very sure no one can break that chain. Not even Pepe the altar boy who's the oldest and is so strong...

Where's the deer coming from?
From the burning hill.
What's it got in its scorched tail?

Hands clasp. The girls twirl around...

Here comes the deer! Here it comes, here it comes!

The little feet whirl around. Girls' feet. Black and white hands join together. Little girls' hands.

There goes the deer...

Luisa Figueroa is the deer. She comes running and tries to break through the center of the circle. The girls stop her by turning around faster and faster. Luisa Figueroa crouches and tries to slip in between the joined arms. The circle stops. Hands clasp even tighter. The chain must not break.

"What's this chain made out of?"

"Gold!"

"Gold, no way!"

"See if you can break it."

Luisa Figueroa leans over two hands clasped tightly. The girls are red-faced with effort, their muscles taut.

"If it's made of gold, you can't break it."

"What's this chain made out of?"

Now she's close to Ana Isabel whose hand is tightly gripping Justina's.

"What's this chain made out of?"

Ana Isabel thinks about little black Eusebio.

"It's made of iron," she answers.

"Made of iron? Go on! It's made out of an ugly dirty arm!"

"What? What did you say? Say it again!"

"Dirty, ugly arm," Luisa Figueroa shouts.

Everything before Ana Isabel's eyes goes blank. Now she's not looking at the circle of girls, not at La Negra Nicasia who's sweeping the yard, not at Cecilia, not at Justina, who's squeezing her hand tenderly. Everything suddenly grows dark and she can barely hear her own gruff voice.

"I'm going to bite you!"

"I'm going to bite you!" Ana Isabel has said, and Luisa Figueroa is crying out loud with a bloody arm. No more chains now. The hands are freed from their grasps.

The gruff voice continues to shout. "I'm going to bite you!" "I'm going to bite you!"

....

In the classroom Ana Isabel sits in front of the desk with her notebook open holding a pencil between her fingers. She has to write "I am not a mad dog" five hundred times. In the lower patio the girls continue playing "The Deer." Their shouts and laughter reach Ana Isabel in the empty room.

Where's the deer coming from?
From the burning hill!

Dirty and ugly...

Everyone tells her she's ugly. People who see her on the street and Esperanza Caldera and Luisa Figueroa. Justina and Cecilia don't say that, but they haven't said she's pretty, either. No one has ever told her she's pretty. No one? Yes, little black Eusebio told her she's pretty and he also promised to give her a treasure. Ana Isabel lay sleepless night after night on account of the treasure, and also because someone had told her she was pretty for the first time... One afternoon, coming home from school on the corner of La Cruz, Eusebio stood with his hands made into fists. Ana Isabel ran to meet him.

Four marbles! Four colored marbles, round and shiny quivered in Eusebio's white palm. Four colored marbles!

Little black Eusebio is the only one who's told her she's pretty. And...who knows? maybe someday he could turn white? Maybe he could be a Prince Charming? He knows so many games, so many songs! Eusebio's palm is white. Ana Isabel remembered how the marbles quivered in it. Could he be turning white? But even if that happened, she could never marry him...

"Alcántara blood will not mix with plebeian blood! We have a very spotless coat-of-arms," Dr. Alcántara is constantly repeating. "And we don't have any money: proof that we're not thieves or scoundrels..."

Doesn't little black Eusebio have a coat-of-arms? Ana Isabel has never asked him, maybe because she knows perfectly well that he doesn't have one. Why doesn't he make one up? It's so easy! The Alcántara coat of arms is in a little square gilt frame that hangs next to the console. On it you can see the helmet, because the Alcántaras were warriors, and bunches of spikes and gold cauldrons on an azure field. Why doesn't he make one up? It could have a shiny black colt with its tail raised up and bunches of blooming melon plants. Her father keeps drawing paper in the display cabinet. When no one is looking she'll take out a sheet and also some colored pencils to make Eusebio a coat-of-arms. For the motto, Eusebio can recite one of his loveliest verses and since he doesn't know how to write, Ana Isabel will do it for him. That day she won't forget to cross her "t's" and make her "o"s nice and round.

"I am not a mad dog. I am not a mad dog..."

Recess is just about over and Ana Isabel hasn't finished writing out her punishment. Maybe they'll keep her writing until six o'clock.

To be forced to write five hundred times—what nonsense. Doesn't she know she's not a mad dog? If she bit Luisa Figueroa it's because she called her ugly. Whenever someone calls Ana Isabel ugly she bites them and whenever she sees a pretty girl she has the urge to bite her and draw blood from her little round arms...

But Ana Isabel won't be sad. Little black Eusebio told her she was pretty. She'll make him a pretty coat-of-arms, and they will walk hand-in-hand, Ana Isabel's thin hand and Eusebio's black one. They'll walk through the fields Ana Isabel likes so much and they'll collect bunches of the lucky flower, purple lantana. And when night falls and the moonlight bathes the dark dirt road, little black Eusebio won't be black, he'll be white, white in the moonlight...

Where's the deer coming from?
From the burning hill
What's it got in its scorched tail?
Let's run and go see...

Who Killed Butterfly?

Little Morning Star and Butterfly had arrived in a cart with their legs tied together. Butterfly was the color of coffee with cream and Little Morning Star was all white, with black legs and a big spot in the middle of her forehead. The smell of manure floated up in the yard. The cows sunk their snouts in the trough and scared the flies away with their tails. Every morning at dawn, Ana Isabel awoke to the mooing of the cows and Balbino's songs.

"Up, Little Morning Star!...up Butterfly!...

Ana Isabel and Jaime, snug and warm, would wake up. Fog covered the rooftops and the dense branches of the guasimo tree were barely visible. A crystal clear silence extended through the hallways. Dust settled on tables, on chairs. The smells of a sleeping household, of warm sheets. Sleepy voices and dead moths stuck to the lamp. In the darkened corridor drops of water mechanically slid over the surface of the clay tank and then they gathered into one shivering drop that falls down slowly. Green ferns peek through between the bars of the fence. Ana Isabel stands back to look at the tank. The clay tank, the tin pitcher whose borders ending in sharp points looks like an old king's crown. The tank continued to sing. First, the big drop, the one who broke through the mirrored surface with a deep sound, then the little ones fall, one after the other, with the sound of twinkling crystals as they take their turns. It always happened the same way. The big drop waited patiently so that they could gather themselves beside it, to allow themselves to fall, majestically, with a solemn air. The small ones followed it, loitering at the same level as the porous stone, splashing the little leaves of the fern as they fell. Ana Isabel held her hand against the body of the tank and its song vibrated through her fingers. What mysterious imp lived in the tank? Small, invisible, full of voices. A dwarf imp, dressed in water, a prisoner in its green cage. A smell of damp valleys, of rainy fields rose from the ferns. The light in the patio crept up to the hall which was still in shadow, filtering in through the window blinds.

"Up, Little Morning Star!... Up, Butterfly...!

She had to cross the dung heap and walk carefully across the yard because of the soapy laundry that was spread out on the floor. And to shelter herself under the eaves when an early morning drizzle fell, thin and white. The door was always half-open, the hinges always squeaked with their out-of-tune sound. The barnyard had been built onto the house with the arrival of the cows. Before that, the door had been shut, with big boards nailed across it. Between the cracks Ana Isabel could glimpse the other side. That's where the islanders lived. The father, a small man with a mustache that fell on either side of his lips. Four little children were lying on the floor, naked and filthy. The mother had white skin scored with tiny wrinkles that buried into her skin when she laughed, showing gums like a newborn's. But Ana Isabel only had eyes for Elisa, the twelve-year-old girl who washed and ironed the neighborhood ladies' laundry. Ana Isabel watched her wring out the big white sheets by hand, spreading them out so they looked like the white carpets in those countries where the snow blankets the earth and the stones in the road. The wind made them wave, the sun bleached them. When they were dry, rough and stiff, Elisa took them off the line one by one and sprinkled them with fresh water before she ironed them. The first day Ana Isabel entered the yard she found it empty and without any voices, very different from when she looked at it from behind the bars where the sheets unfurled their great wings in the wind.

Who Killed Butterfly?

A lean-to sheltered the cows. Ana Isabel's mother washed out the buckets in the faucet connected to the pipe. Balbino was kneeling, milking the cows. Little Morning Star and Butterfly folded their legs and were mooing softly. Balbino took the udders in his calloused hands. Udders of satiny skin. Milk came out in streaming fountains, in thin strands that crisscrossed in the air and fell into the bucket of warm foaming milk. From time to time the cows mooed and closed their eyes and opened them again and stared at the beams in the roof. Ana Isabel dipped her fingertips in the foam, caressed the cow's hides and jumped away when they suddenly kicked.

"Girl, you're just asking for the cows to kick you! Ana Isabel, for the love of God, let Balbino milk the cows, it's getting late!"

When the buckets were full, Ana Isabel's mother adjusted the lids and Balbino tied the buckets to either side of the mule who was waiting patiently at the door of the yard.

"Your mother, she sells milk?" Esperanza Caldera asked Ana Isabel as she chewed licorice.

"What, she sells milk?" Luisa Figueroa asked in turn.

"Yes, she does, and what about it?" Ana Isabel replied with her eyes shining darkly.

"C'mon, girl, don't get so upset. It's just a question. Does she sell milk?"

Ana Isabel turns her back on them and walks toward the patio where they are playing jump rope.

"Ana Isabel, do you want to come into the circle?" Justina smiles as the rope quickly slides between her fingers.

"I don't feel like playing today, Justina."

Cecilia approaches her with thoughtful tenderness.

"Are you sick? What's wrong?"

"Nothing. I just don't feel like playing, that's all."

Maquini surci, maniqui sursa...
Give me the ring, give me the ring
That's in your hand...

Justina's crystalline voice can be heard under the afternoon sky. The leaves are beginning to turn yellow. The summer burns the earth dry, tightening the rose buds. Ana Isabel sits in the corner of the patio. The honeysuckle creeps up to the roof and between the tiles in aromatic bunches.

She thinks about her mother's hands, rough, red, and the trembling water that covers them. In the hot manure with their acid fermenting smell. The recently mown grass the cows graze, the warm milk, covered with little bubbles that burst in the breeze.

"Up, Little Morning Star... up Butterfly!..."

"Mama, when are they coming to take the cows away?"

"But child, why would you want them to take the cows away?"

"I want them to take them away, mama."

"Stop being naughty, Ana Isabel. First you fall in love with the cows and now you don't like them. Look, child, the cows help us stay alive. You already know that. So they are here to stay. What a strange girl you are, good Lord!"

Ana Isabel doesn't get up at dawn like she did before. Jaime calls her and she turns her head to the wall, pretending to be asleep.

"Ana Isabel, get up. Balbino's here!"

"Leave her alone, my son, now she hates the cows. Good Lord, what a strange girl she is!"

From her bed, Ana Isabel listens to Balbino's song, the water running out of the faucet, the clanging of the buckets.

Who Killed Butterfly?

"Ana Isabel, Butterfly is sick!" Jaime hurriedly rushes into the room.

"She's sick. Butterfly is sick, Ana Isabel!"

Ana Isabel leaps out of bed. Her white nightgown covers her knees and slides down her legs and to her ankles until it reaches the floor. She doesn't look at the tank. Her feet getting tangled in the soapy clothes, she trips against the door whose hinges squeak with their harsh, discordant tune.

Butterfly is lying on the floor with her legs doubled over and her head nodding forward. Balbino is next to her, passing his hand across her belly with an unexpected gentleness.

"Bad grass, missus, bad grass she ate... Now she'll get better."

"Ana Isabel, what are you doing here barefoot and in your nightgown? You're going to catch cold. Go get dressed, child."

But Ana Isabel clings to her mother's skirts with trembling hands.

"It's that... is she... is she..."

She doesn't want to say what has crossed her mind. What does she know about death? Ana Isabel? A word that is spoken in a lowered voice that makes faces sad. Tolling bells, leafless flowers in the hallway.

Mrs. Alcántara feels the little hand grasping her skirts.

"No, my child. Go get dressed," she responds softly. Butterfly will get better. Come..."

Yes, it's all her fault. Didn't she want the cows to go away? Butterfly is going to die. She will be still, stiff, her eyes cold.

"Are you awake, Ana Isabel? What are you talking about? Be quiet and go to sleep."

"It's...it's Butterfly, mama..."

69

"I already told you she'll get better, don't worry, sleep well."

She slept a dull, heavy sleep, punctuated by labored breathing. In the middle of her dream, Butterfly was growing bigger. Her shiny back reached up to the beams in the ceiling and her head reached out, her ears open wide like giant lilies. A loud and unceasing mooing could be heard from afar, further away than the patio, crossing the hallways, the dark corridor, crossing the veranda and reaching her room, right up to her own bed. Ana Isabel felt squeezed in between the waves of sound that reached even closer to her, while Butterfly continued to grow, breaking through the ceiling and reaching further with her head to the sky, next to the clouds. When she woke up, sweat was running down her forehead and her clenched hands were grasping the sheets. Butterfly was not getting better. Her legs were swollen and her udders were hanging loose. Plasters of nightshade, Balbino advised. They ground the mixture in the mortar near the stove and soaked the animal's legs with the thick juice. She turned her head and her gaze was heavy and frightened.

"Why isn't she getting up?"

"Why not, cause she's sick. Can't you see?"

"Ana Isabel, it's time for school. Go on, when you get back, she'll be better."

At school Ana Isabel jumped at the least sound. The sound of a doorknocker, moved by the wind, made her shiver.

"Ana Isabel Alcántara! Pay attention!"

The teacher is reading them the story of Jacob and Esau.

"...and then," the teacher continued, Jacob covered himself with a goat's hide to fool his father."

A goat's hide is rough, and Butterfly is soft, soft as satin, smooth as white wax. And a spot in the middle of her forehead, and dark polished legs. A star in the middle of her forehead. The stomach continued to swell. Thick saliva was coming out of her snout, her tongue was turning purple. Ana Isabel comes nearer and offers her a bucket of fresh water, but Butterfly barely moves her head and wets the tips of her snout.

"What if we try mustard plasters?" Balbino suggested.

Mrs. Alcántara moistens the compresses in the boiling liquid. Butterfly remains still upon contact with the heat. Flies are buzzing all around her. A big fly with fragile transparent wings lands on her back. The ears are turned back, the legs doubled over and stuck to the ground. Little shudders run through her flanks from time to time.

"Is she cold, Balbino?"

"No, girl, what cold? She's sick, can't you see?"

"Ana Isabel, come and eat. You can't spend your whole life next to that cow, my little child, it's not good for you..."

Sitting at the table, father, mother, children silent. Mrs. Alcántara sighs and breaks off a piece of bread and brings it distractedly to her lips.

"Go on, eat, my little one. And you, Jaime, aren't you eating either?"

But the mother doesn't insist and the soup grows cold in the bowl.

"Is Butterfly very sick, Federico?"

"Well, Balbino must do something. They're not going to let her die, I think."

"We'll do what we can," the mother softly replies.

Butterfly is getting worse. She's barely breathing with a rasp that enlarges her neck and she's foaming at the mouth. The shiny eyes are inert. Ana Isabel comes closer and looks at them, like two little mirrors, her little face, her braids tied with red ribbons. The afternoon slowly fades. Stars are appearing in the corners of the sky. A spider is busily weaving between the beams...

They took her away in a cart, the same cart she had come in on. But now her belly was not moving, her eyes were staring straight ahead. Her legs inert, stiff, shrunken. Her back covered with flies. Ana Isabel watched her leave as she clung to her mother's skirts, her eyes dry.

"What can we do, child! She couldn't get better. Come with me, don't look at her any more. Don't cry, Ana Isabel." The reddened fingers caress the blonde head. The breeze, forecasting rain whirls around the stones and lifts the dust. Two black birds fly off...

Not much later, Little Morning Star would also leave. Mrs. Alcántara swept the yard clean, washed the metal buckets for the last time with water from the faucet. Moving slowly, pausing with quiet resignation, she walked Balbino to the doorway.

"Just one cow won't be worth it, Balbino. And so many haven't paid up. Maybe some other time..."

The islanders returned. All day long Ana Isabel heard the sound of the hammer nailing the boards back up. Elisa began once again to wring the sheets, to hang them on the clothesline, white and damp. But Ana Isabel no longer looked through the cracks at the other side. She stayed near the door hinges, leaning against the boards. In the corridor the tank continued to sing its song, day and night. Big drops fell, small ones filled the tank. The ferns grew green with their scent of woodsy mornings.

The recess bell rang late for Ana Isabel who had been waiting for it since she got to school. The girls were running into the patio dazed, like birds who'd just escaped from their cages. They soon formed small groups and games were organized.

"Hey, I've got to talk to you."

Esperanza Caldera looks at Ana Isabel's determined face. "With me? What do you have to say to me?"

"Come," Ana Isabel replies tersely.

"And where do you want me to go?"

"Come," Ana Isabel replies again. "To the downstairs patio where we'll be alone."

"But the teacher doesn't want us to go to the downstairs patio."

"But I want to." And Ana Isabel's eyes grow grey and steely.

The two girls silently start climbing down the steep stairs. It's cold below. The floor is slippery, big greenish splotches cover the cement.

Ana Isabel stopped in the shadiest part of the patio. In the corner are broken baskets, the ironing board leaning against the wall, suitcases covered with dust and cobwebs.

"Now," Ana Isabel says dryly," you're going to pay."

"Pay for what? But, Ana Isabel, what's with you?"

Esperanza Caldera started shaking. They were alone in the corner of the patio shaded by the wall of the house next door. A damp smell, of still water. The girls' song could be heard in the distance. A weak afternoon sun was spreading its rays on the top of the eaves...

"You're going to pay."

Esperanza Caldera watches as Ana Isabel straightens up in front of her, as though she had suddenly grown. She's always looked down on little Ana Isabel, small and pale. But now that white face, drained of blood! Those lips pressed together!

"You killed her and you're gonna to pay for it. You killed her! You! You!"

"But who did I kill? I didn't kill anybody! You're crazy, Ana Isabel. Let go of me!"

Trembling she leaned against the ironing board. Ana Isabel moves even closer. Esperanza Caldera can feel her breath close to her and she sees the flashing in her eyes.

"Let you go? You're going to pay! I had it in for you since the day she died. Because you killed her. Take this! Take this! You killed her! You! You!"

When the teacher comes running down the stairs, Ana Isabel is still hitting Esperanza Caldera, who's lying on the ground with her face covered with blood.

"What's this all about, girls? Ana Isabel, snap out of it. What's all this? Good heavens!"

The other girls also go running down the stairs. The teacher pulls them apart. She takes Esperanza Caldera in her arms and slowly climbs the stairs one by one. Ana Isabel marches behind her like an automaton, her arms stiff at her sides. Standing before the teacher's desk, before her stern gaze, she still acts as though she is sleepwalking. The teacher violently shakes her by her shoulders.

"Speak up, answer me! Say something! Why did you do it? Do you realize what you've done? Are you out of your mind?"

Ana Isabel stares at the table, at the map of Venezuela, the inkwell, the ruler...

"You can do whatever you like to me," she replies with a blank voice. "But she's the one who killed her..."

And there, coming from afar, something quiets down deep inside Ana Isabel. A sad mooing, the smell of dung and cowpats, songs in the morning mist...

"Up, Little Morning Star!... Up, Butterfly!..."

The Piñata Party

Ana Isabel, come curl your straight hair or you won't look nice for the piñata party. Ana Isabel runs to the patio to look for rose leaves. Hard green leaves she crushes to make the juice to curl her hair. The piñata party is this afternoon. She hasn't been able to eat a bite just thinking about the piñata party. By now the clay pot has been decorated with crepe paper in different colors and curled by scissors; it's already filled with candy and cookies. Of course she'll be the one to break the piñata. What is she going to wear? She'll have to go again in the same old thing, because even after they promised to buy her a new one after exams were over, they haven't. Luisa Figueroa and Esperanza Caldera will wear silk dresses with satin sashes. And Justina will surely wear her pink dress, a dress so lovely you feel like eating it. Everyone will be wearing new clothes and she herself always in the same dress...

But she'll be the one who'll break the piñata, because she runs faster than the others and is stronger than them. She'll take hold of the pole, also decorated like the piñata with curled crepe paper and even though she'll be blindfolded, she'll be confident and then bang, bang... the piñata will drop to the ground. Ana Isabel will throw herself on it and will pick up heaps of cookies and candy... Yes, it will be she who'll break the piñata. She already told Carmencita and Perico. Carmencita didn't know what a piñata was; she's never been to a piñata party, has Carmencita.

"So why don't you come with me this afternoon? It's going to be over there, behind the square, at Teresita Rodríquez's house. The little girl who plays Four Plants with us, remember?" But Carmencita doesn't answer. Her eyes are wide open and she's staring at Ana Isabel in amazement.

"Put on a clean dress, comb your hair out, but not in pigtails, because respectable girls don't wear pigtails. Wear your hair loose and put a ribbon in it. I've got a blue one I can give you. Of course you're going! I'll be there standing by the window waiting for you, alright?"

Ana Isabel hasn't been able to eat her lunch thinking about the piñata party.

"If you go on like that, not eating, I'm not going to let you go to any more parties, Ana Isabel! Just look at this child, any time she's about to go somewhere, she doesn't eat a bite all day. Learn from your brother."

What time is it? It's one o'clock. One o'clock and the piñata party is at three o'clock. Oh, how slowly the hours go by!... Ana Isabel walks through the patio. She throws bread crumbs to the little fish. She looks at the ants busily come and go. She climbs to the top of the roof, then climbs down. She looks at herself in the mirror, her hair is tied up in fourteen curlers. But her hair is still damp and if it doesn't dry it won't be curly. She'll have to sit in the sun to dry her hair. Ana Isabel heads back to the patio and lies down next to the begonia plant. The plant is in bloom. Little pink flowers with small yellow dots at the center. Ana Isabel likes to eat the begonia, they taste like sharp, tangy candy, those candies that look like marbles. How hard the ground is! Hard and dry because it hasn't rained. Ana Isabel likes to lie on the ground. But, would she also like to sleep on the ground? Yes, to sleep without her soft warm bed? To have to sleep on the ground like Pepe the altar boy, wrapped up in newspapers when it's cold...

No, she wouldn't like to sleep on the ground. And surely Pepe doesn't like to, either. Maybe Pepe wants a little bed like hers, soft and warm. Her father bought her the little bed and Pepe doesn't have a father. Well, he does, but it's as if he doesn't. Ana Isabel thought that Pepe didn't have a father. In the San José del Ávila slum, there is only Auntie Rosario, Pepe's mother. Rosario who's always sick, always coughing and she's so thin that Ana Isabel thinks she won't be able to stand up for long. And yet, Rosario works so hard! She grinds the corn for the arepas and makes the home-made sweets that Pepe sells in the afternoon, majarete and coconut preserves. Ana Isabel would like to eat the majarete and coconut preserves Rosario makes but Mrs. Alcántara says that those are dirty sweets, made in a slum that's a pigsty. One day Pepe gave her a little cup of majarete and some coconut preserves wrapped in orange leaves. Ana Isabel ate them secretly and the next day she came down with a fever and a stomachache.

"Who knows what junk from the street she ate," Mrs. Alcántara repeated.

Yes, Ana Isabel forgot that Pepe had a father, but one afternoon when they were playing Four Plants in the little square, a man came by wearing alpargatas, dressed in khaki and wearing a straw hat. Pepe stopped running and with a solemn face asked him for his blessing.

"God bless you, alright, wow, look at him, he's becoming a man...and he's gonna be as manly as me."

And the man glances at Ana Isabel with malice.

"Take this bolívar to your mom, OK?"

The man kept laughing and Pepe stood still in the middle of the square with the coin in his hand.

"Who's that?" Ana Isabel asked.

"My father."

"Your father? So why doesn't he live with you?"

"That's his problem. What do I know? None of my business, none of my business."

And Ana Isabel thinks that the poor, the truly poor, not like her, not like Ana Isabel, but the poor like Perico and

Carmencita, like Eusebio, Pepe the altar boy, and Petrica, Domitila's daughter, and Eladio, the one who lives down by the ravine, the really poor people almost never have a father. Petrica, Domitila's daughter, doesn't have a father, neither does Eladio, or Eusebio, or Encarnacíon, Concha's son. The poor don't have a father, they only have a mother. The mother who cleans, does the laundry, who makes the arepas, who carries the water... Why don't the poor have a father? Ana Isabel had asked Gregoria. Gregoria is not usually tongue-tied and she always dispels Ana Isabel's doubts. But today Gregoria was silent, blowing over the red-hot coals that lifted up a cloud of ashes that settled on Ana Isabel's golden hair.

"Is Rosario married? And Domitila and Concha? Why don't the fathers of poor people live with them?"

"Look, girl, you need money to get married, and men don't marry no poor women. So why go home to them? Why the heck?"

"But how can they have children if they're not married?"

This time Gregoria was silent. The coals grew hotter and hotter and the straw hat that fanned the flames folded over, swayed and caught fire on the stove in a burst of flames, lighting up Ana Isabel's small delicate face.

"My child, come get dressed, it's two thirty already." Two thirty! She'll have to hurry and get dressed or she'll be late for the piñata party. Jaime's almost dressed already, he only needs to tie his shoelaces and he's busy doing it by himself, because he's a man. A grown-up man!

"Don't undo your curlers yet, Ana Isabel, not until the last minute so your hair will be curlier." But Ana Isabel is eager to look at herself in the mirror with her hair in curls and with the moiré ribbon. Her dress is so white; it smells clean, of soap, it has that warm, just-pressed smell. Mrs. Alcántara had washed it herself and ironed the lace and the inserts one by one. Ana Isabel, looking at herself in her fresh dress and curly hair, almost dares to call herself pretty. At the Rodríquez household they've cleared the hallway and hung the piñata from a little beam. The parlor furniture has been pushed up against the veranda; Teresita's grandmother is sitting in a big armchair. She's so old she's almost blind, her little eyes are watery and her chin is trembling. She's sitting in the seat of honor in front of the veranda's door. She doesn't want to miss out on the piñata party. "Teresa, ma'am, be careful with those boys, they are so big they might hit you with the pole. Yes, it would be better if you moved inside a tiny bit more, mother, you are old and the boys don't know how to handle that blessed piñata."

"No darling. What are you talking about. Let me stay here."

"Ah, the Alcántaras are here. What a handsome boy! Look, mother, what a handsome boy! Put on your glasses so you can see him better. These are Federico Alcántara's children. Poor Federico, always so sick..."

"Teresita, show Ana Isabel your presents and then come back because we are about to break the piñata." The parlor windows are wide open and outside children are looking in, hanging on to the bars. Following the children are dirty barefoot women holding babies in their arms. They all want to see the piñata break. The foyer is also full of ragged children who reach in and poke their heads toward the hallway. The children run through the patio among the crotons and many kinds of rose bushes, trampling the violets that border the strips of grass.

Mrs. Rodríquez is holding a handkerchief in one hand and a pole with a piece of curled paper on its tip and is having the children line up.

"You're first, my love. Come here, my darling, so I can blindfold you."

"Spin him around three times!"

"One, two, three!"

Bang! Bang!

"Higher, no, lower! Hit it hard, Enriqueta... Hit it hard!"

"Now it's Felipon's turn. I'll bet Felipon will bring it down. Come on, Felipon, hit it, hit it hard!"

"Careful, child, stand back!"

"Move away from there, Ana Isabel, or you're going to get hit!"

Though the clay pot was deliberately purchased with a crack in it for the piñata, it's still in one piece. The crepe paper is hanging in shreds and it's starting to look sad. Esperanza Caldera who almost always breaks the piñata hasn't been able to do it this time.

Luisa Figueroa has also hit it many times and managed to make the pot lean over, but it didn't break.

"Now, Ana Isabel. Now you, Ana Isabel!"

How dark it is. Why did they have to put the blindfold on so tight? If only she could see a little, just a tiny bit.

"Don't cheat, Ana Isabel! Ana Isabel is cheating, she's lifting the blindfold."

"Come here, Ana Isabel..."

Mrs. Rodríquez ties the blindfold even tighter over Ana Isabel's eyes. The shadows fill with bright stars, with little gold and red worms that grow larger and larger and form big circles.

"Three spins, three spins!"

"One, two, three..."

And Ana Isabel gropes along in her shadows with the pole in her hand and her head held high."

Bang! Bang!

"Higher! Higher!... No over there, a tiny bit more!... A little lower!"

"There! There! Hit it, Ana Isabel, hit it hard! There, there..."

A shower of cookies, candies, pieces of crockery. The children squeeze in, push each other, drag each other, laugh and cry with their mouths full.

"I got more than you."

"Whadda you mean, you got nothing."

"I got nothing, so what's all this?"

"Did you get a peach, Ana Isabel?"

"A peach, and candy and little cookies... I got more than anyone and besides it was me who broke it."

"Let's play The Deer"

"No, Doñana is better."

"Who's gonna be Doñana?"

"Me,"

"Me"

Let's go to the lemon-balm grove
To see Doñana cut parsley

"They're looking for you, Ana Isabel."

They're looking for her? Who could be looking for her? Maybe they want to congratulate her for breaking the piñata. Maybe she'll get a prize. A story by Calleja, a plastic doll, a top.

"Ana Isabel's eyes are shining and her cheeks are flushed.

"Who could it be?"

"Carmencita..."

How could she have forgotten that she'd promised to wait for Carmencita. Carmencita is there at the door. Her hair is loose, black hair, silky, falling over her shoulders in dark waves, a blue ribbon, Ana Isabel's ribbon, wrapped around one of the curls. She's wearing a percale dress and big shoes with scuffed toes.

"Come in, Carmencita, come in." Ana Isabel leads her by the hand and drags her toward the hallway. Carmencita doesn't dare take a step. She's shy. She's played with all these girls in the square in the afternoons but they don't look the same. They are all dressed up! Here comes Mrs. Rodríquez. Carmencita wants to run away, but her feet feel heavy, like stones.

"Come here, Ana Isabel..."

Mrs. Rodríquez leads Ana Isabel to a corner of the dining room and speaks to her in a low voice, very hurriedly. Yes, she knows that Carmencita is a good girl, but she's not Teresita's friend. Today is her saint's feast day and her father has given the party for her little friends. So that all of them can have fun and play nicely together.

"What do you mean, she's not Teresita's friend? But she plays with her every day in the square..."

"Yes, she plays in the square...but that's not the same thing. Besides, we don't know who her mother and father are..."

"Of course she's got a mother. And her father? You don't think I don't know who he is? It's Ruperto, the coal man!"

"Yes, my child, but she can't stay at the party. She just can't, my child. When you are older you'll understand."

Carmencita hasn't moved. Her silky hair shines in the orangey light of the afternoon and casts blue shadows on the white percale dress.

"When you are older you will understand..."

Ana Isabel isn't grown up yet, but she understands. She'll have to tell her to leave. But she won't be able to. The words dry up between her lips just like on exam days.

"Carmencita..."

Ana Isabel takes Carmencita timidly by the hand. Carmencita's hand is cold and trembling.

"I want to go home."

The girls approach and begin to gather around Carmencita.

"What's going on?"

"A little black girl that Ana Isabel wanted to let in," says Luisa Figueroa.

"Little black girl? But Carmencita is white!"

"I want to go home."

"Wait, Carmencita. Take...candies, cookies... Take more, candies, take..."

And the peach? Will she also have to give her the peach? How warm and sweet-smelling the peach skin is. It has a soft, fuzzy skin she wants to caress. It's been a while since Ana Isabel has eaten a peach. She's never seen one like this one, so pretty and rosy. She's sure it will be sweet and juicy, so much so that when she bites into it, the juice will run down her face, will fill her hands... But Carmencita's eyes are so sad.

"You've never eaten a peach? Carmencita, look, this one's nice and big. Take it."

The afternoon glows in reds and purples. A sad afternoon. Carmencita runs in the afternoon. She runs through the narrow streets, through the cobblestone streets. There's the square, she'll be there soon. There are the treetops. The bells are already ringing in Mary's month. Mary's month is May, the month the flowers called "marías" are in bloom and the grass is carpeted with the little red buds that tumble down in little circles. There are the treetops. Carmencita heads there running. Now she's climbing the stairs, now she's crossing the square, stepping on the grass, on the red maría flowers and the cottony bits from the kopak tree. Dusk descends darkly down from Mount Ávila, from the church tower, from the tall treetops. Dusk descends, it gathers on the grass and encircles the square, little Candelaria Square. Dusk descends and a broken-hearted little girl runs in the dusk.

Delirium

"Come on, child! Open your mouth. Stop misbehaving, Ana Isabel. Learn from your brother who doesn't make a fuss when he has to take his medicine. Why do you make things so hard? Come on, open your mouth."

But Ana Isabel keeps her teeth clenched and her mouth closed.

"Why did you stuff yourself with cocoanut preserve? I told you a thousand times that those sweets are filthy. It's your own fault you got sick. Come on, my little one, take the laxative. Don't cry, Ana Isabel. Crying won't solve anything. Take the medicine."

A half-light barely lights the room. It's daytime and outside the sun is shining brightly, but the half-light barely lets familiar objects be seen.

"All right, I'll have to force it down you. I'm going to call your father so he can pry your mouth open..."

The glass, the spoon, the orange slice.... All are bathed in a weak and endearing light. In the house, silence surrounds everything, even her mother's voice seems muffled by the stillness.

"Who knows if it's chicken pox this girl's got. That's what comes of playing with those dirty, ragged children. Carmencita, the coalman's daughter, Estefanía says she's got chicken pox and you play with her."

Chicken pox? Does she have it? How cold she feels and how hot her hands are! Chicken pox is like smallpox. Your body gets covered with big red sores. Eladio's aunt came down with smallpox and now her face is covered with deep scars. And she's ugly, very ugly, is Eladio's aunt.

Delirium

Down by where Eladio lives, once they get sick, they die. Anita, a very pale little girl who lived next to Eladio died one morning just as the sun was beginning to warm things up. Eladio told that to Ana Isabel when he asked her for flowers for the little dead girl. Ana Isabel cut heliotrope and marigolds and even a rose, without first asking her mother for permission. How lovely and how big the room is. How the furniture creaks. It's almost like something is living inside it. But what's that sound? It's not the water, or the water falling in the tank. It's louder, harsh, heavy, like earth. A shutter opened high up in the window. She'll have to lean over in bed so she can see the patio. The patio with its little fountain and the cement Cupid in the middle. And the colorful little fish Ana Isabel and Jaime have fun throwing breadcrumbs to. The patio with its red bougainvillea so red it seems like it's on fire. And the sago palm and the guava and that tall one that is chili pepper. Outside the sun is shining brightly and the water in the fountain must be warm. How delicious it would be to plunge her hands, her burning hands into the warm water. To crush the water lilies which make a small popping noise and frighten the little fish sleeping beneath them. How delicious it would be to bathe at the rim of the fountain like she and Jaime do when it's been washed and the water is clean and bright. To bathe with the calabash and wash her body with fresh clear water. To put her hands in the warm water. To watch the little fish tremble and shiver. To feel them slide across her thin warm slender fingers. To watch them rise up wet and shiny. To catch them gently with tenderness and spread them out on her fiery hands. One afternoon Ana Isabel had held a little fish in her hand. Pantaleón the pharmacist had given it to her. Pantaleón, always thin and sleepy, among white jars with words in Latin written on them. The pharmacy had a wooden counter and was always full of men and women who came looking for medicine. Dirty women, flea-ridden, with pieces of flannel covering their cheeks, who were dying of pain with toothaches and asked for creosote oil. There were also little children who ran around and ducked and slid under Pantaleón's counter and pulled on his smock and he shouted to scare them away but not without first giving them a round yellow gumball the children chewed greedily. Every day Pantaleón raised the screen to let in Mr. Ramírez who lived on the corner of El Pantanal, who dressed in black and had gold teeth and a wart on his nose. Mr. Ramírez came to use the phone.

Ana Isabel would also duck and slip under the counter to watch Pantaleón with his watery red eyes pour green liquids into big tall glasses. Sometimes the pharmacy was empty. No one banged on the counter to be waited on. It was the siesta hour, the time when in the heat of the day the trolley was empty and the driver turned the steering wheel while he sounded the bell. Then Pantaleón would climb on a high stool, adjust his glasses as he yawned and write out labels in his beautiful cursive handwriting. He wrote evocative names, colorful names, like the stories in *A Thousand and One Nights*.

"Tincture of Lobelia..." "Lavender Oil..."

Ana Isabel, leaning on the counter, closed her eyes. The smell of pyroxylin, iodine, chloroform... The smell of bandages and wounds. Falls from skates, bumps on heads... Ana Isabel closed her eyes and opened them again to look at the containers of sugar, rubber gum paste, pulpy and hot. The fish Pantaleón had given her was made of gelatin. Red gelatin, transparent, so much so that Ana Isabel could look through it and see Pantaleón rubbing his eyes. A gelatin fish! Ana Isabel rubbed her hands one against the other to warm them, following Pantaleón's advice, and then she placed the little fish over her warm hands. How it raised its tail and moved its head with its little round green eyes!

"Don't jump around like that, child. Lie still."

Delirium

Jumping, sliding, like the fish! A little gelatin fish! Grab it, Ana Isabel. Little brown fish, silver tail, blue eyes, little red mouth...

How dark the room is! She'll have to lean over in bed to see the patio. But it's not the patio she sees through the shutter, it's the rooftop from the house next door. It's the magnolia tree in bloom. Vicente told her the buds are thickening and when the prettiest and most fragrant flower opens up, it will be for Ana Isabel. He'll have to climb very high to reach it. Very high, Ana Isabel! See how the wind moves it, how it bends it. And it's the wind that brings puffs of scent, a scent so intense it makes her feel light-headed and drowsy... And its milky petals grow, its fleshy petals, and the birds also grow. There are huge birds in the treetops!

But it's not the magnolia tree, it's the tree in the little square that's still snow white and it's cold. Down below it's sunny and they are playing Bogey Man. Bogey Man's coming to get you!

"Careful, or you'll fall!" Perico fell while he was playing Bogey Man and they took him bleeding to the pharmacy. Pantaleón bandaged him and Perico couldn't run for many days. Sitting in the shade, on old rough roots, he had to watch the others jumping around...

But it's not snow, it's cotton. It's the cotton from the tree, and Ana Isabel's hands, eyes and mouth are full and she can't see... But she listens, she listens to the wind that roars and whistles. There goes Carmencita running. Ana Isabel yells out but she has no voice. Her voice lingers high above, among the branches, in the snow in the night. Dark feverish night. Night of hot, burning body, of sunless eyes. Where is the sun? Carmencita is back and she's sitting on the grass, next to the brown dirt. But Eusebio is here. He's singing. What is Eusebio singing? He sings a song that grows louder in the wind. A song of the sea. Ana Isabel hasn't been to the sea but Eusebio is singing about the sea with its fish, seaweed and resonant shells...

"Child, lie still! Keep your hands still, Ana Isabel!"

Her hands. Her hands that can never be still. Her hands that throb, that shake. Her hands that look for clumps of earth and throw smooth pebbles. Her hands that caress her biggest doll named Frou-Frou who has patent leather shoes with silver buckles...

"Don't move around so much, Ana Isabel! Stop kicking, child! Keep your legs still!"

Her nimble, restless legs! The legs she runs to the ravine and down the gully with. The gully is narrow but when it rains it fills up and becomes so beautiful, so much so that Ana Isabel tells herself it's a river and she imagines she's crossing a bridge as she skips across the rocks slippery with moss. Higher up is the savannah with its tall grass full of yellow flowers and colorful butterflies. In the ravine purslane grows and Ana Isabel lies face up looking at the sky until she's dizzy. When a strong breeze blows it's full of kites with stars, moons and irregular triangles that were cut out with scissors. Eladio's aunt, who has a harsh voice, shouts calling for Eladio and he climbs up the ravine throwing rocks and trampling on the vines.

"Come, my child, open your mouth!... Suck on the orange. Oranges, green oranges, yellow. Orange candy. Round oranges. The earth is round like an orange. Orangey like the sun shining on the howler monkeys. Is it raining? When it rains the rainbow comes out. You can't see it through the shutter, because Pantaleón is there. Pantaleón has an enormous face, immense, that takes up the entire width of the shutter. His eyes are wide open and he's staring at Ana Isabel. Huge, watery eyes. He's crying. He's shedding big shiny tears like the fireworks they set off in the square on the nights of the retreat and they climb high up high up next to the church tower and

Delirium

then go off. But Pantaleón isn't crying, he's laughing and he opens his mouth so wide that it looks like a dark deep tunnel. A tunnel that's very dark through which a track runs. "Clickity clack, clickity clack, the train runs down the track..." "Clickity clack, clickity clack, the train runs down the track..." "Clickity clack, clickity clack, the train runs down the track..." "The night is dark" Estefanía sings. "I'm afraid, Estefanía!" This girl and her terrors!... It's the devil, the devil who's coming to take her away. The devil is approaching the shutter!

"You're perspiring so much, my child! Sleep so you can get over this fever! I'll sing you "The Little Pigs..."

It must be night outside. Cold, blue night. Big night on the patio spilling over the fountain. A dusting of moon over the sago palm. Smaller night in her room, in her soft bed. Smaller night that falls in the hollow of her closed hand.

"You are soaked with sweat, Ana Isabel.... Sleep, my child, sleep..."

"There go the little pigs to the cane fields.
Tie them down, boy, tie them down, boy
Or they'll run away..."

Little Black Eusebio Died

"Watch out, you'll fall, Ana Isabel! That girl's legs are unsteady after her illness." Ana Isabel walks one step at a time. She's already at the door to the veranda. A few more steps and she'll be able to grab hold of the finial on her mother's headboard. One step, one more, a little one. She's regaining her confidence. How long her legs are! How she's grown! Her mother is right.

"While she was sick, this girl's shot up!"

The door to the veranda is open wide and the patio is drenched in sunlight, a hot sun that sears the earth and shrivels the leaves of the magnolia until they are scorched and red. Ana Isabel is walking slowly as though she's afraid to get there. Now she's next to the bed. Now with her hands she is touching the headboard carved with leaves, fruits and round and symmetrical arabesques. The light strikes the wood burnished with copper-colored polished reflections. Ana Isabel looks at her hands. Have her hands also grown? Were they always like this, so long and slender? And the rosy fingernails that appear at their fingertips, like Amelia's, Cecilia's sister, who spends hours polishing them with a chamois cloth. Of course she's grown. Her head now reaches the top of the headboard. Surely she must be taller than Cecilia and Justina and even Esperanza Caldera who thinks that no one will ever be taller than her.

"Are you going to stay lying in bed, Ana Isabel? Didn't I tell you to go out into the patio to get a little sun? Darn, this child, from the minute she gets up she starts disobeying…"

Ana Isabel is still, with her back to the patio. She looks at the wick work bedspread her mother crocheted as she sat by the lamp in the dining room. The big bed! Has

Little Black Eusebio Died

Ana Isabel grown so much that she's starting to remember when she was younger? The big bed! Filled with mystery for her and Jaime. In the early mornings they would wake up and run barefoot on the cement. "Just one more tiny minute, dearest pretty mommy. Just a tiny bit more!"

"But it's time for you to get up, children. And your father is taking his bath. I have to go boil the milk for breakfast..."

But Ana Isabel and Jaime moved closer to their mother's warmth; morning descended over the patio with its reds and mauves. The birds pecked at the guavas and shook their wings before flying from one branch to another. The rooster from Otilia's house sang out in a croaky, tired crow. A rooster...a cowardly and aristocratic rooster that swaggered in the yard, snatching worms from the chickens. Estefanía carried water in the jug. Carts were crossing the street and soon you would hear the hoofs of the bread seller's donkey and hear him pounding on the top of the barrel with a wooden stick.

"Bread! Bread!

"Come get it now, the bread is here. It's almost six o'clock."

Mother would get up and then the big house came alive. Then it became a river, the pillows became a canoe and she and Jaime flowed down the river splashing around going after alligators and water snakes.

"Watch out, the snake's gonna get you. Get out of the way, the caiman's gonna get you..."

They twisted the sheets and rolled them up near their necks and around their arms.

"The snake's got you, the snake's grabbed you..."

Other times the bed became an ocean, the Caribbean. Ana Isabel and Jaime were pirates, the Black, Red and Yellow Pirate...the storm was approaching, the wind was roaring, the waves were pounding and roiling.

Ana Isabel: A Respectable Girl

"We're going to capsize! To port! To starboard!"

"Shipwreck! Shipwreck!"

"But children, you're going to break the bedsprings! With you two around things won't last long in this house. Get down from there and get up it's already six thirty."

Jaime ran away and Ana Isabel hid her head under the sheets and held her breath. Her mother went to the kitchen to light the stove. Ana Isabel listened to the machete chopping wood. The sun had risen so everything was bright. Ana Isabel turned her gaze to the patio and then to the roof. When it rained, the roof leaked and they had to put a pewter washtub on the floor to collect the water that fell from above. The leaks stained the ceiling with large dark stains so when they dried the ceiling was like a map with rivers, mountains, unfamiliar monsters that grimaced and little shapes that smiled roguishly. Ana Isabel, from the bed, with her eyes fixed on the ceiling forgot all about her mother, the patio, her little brother Jaime, the relentless hands of the clock that fatefully marked the time for school.

In the middle of the ceiling there was a big lake with swans, crocodiles and big rocks. An elephant was rolling an apple around in its trunk, like the one she'd seen in the circus when her father took her one morning. And the clown's face with its toothless smile, just like Pantaleón the pharmacist's. And the bony, skinny dog bigger than Chucuto, no doubt, but smaller than Bob, Justina's dog. Its ears were still and its tongue was hanging out. After it rained, Ana Isabel scanned the ceiling to see "what had come out." One afternoon, after a strong downpour, the elephant spread out so much that it also became a lake but next to it appeared a parrot on the rim of a hoop, just like the one in the corner grocery store that squawked at all the passersby.

Ruuun! Ruuun!

The big bed! Ana Isabel wants to lie there like she used to, to snuggle up like when she was little, to feel her mother's warmth, to hear Jaime's laughter. She can't, with her legs, or her trembling hands. She can't open her eyes because the sun shines on her and the wind pushes her hair back and chills the tip of her nose.

"Go on, my child, go get a little sun and I'll bring you your lunch. Don't forget it's the first day you're going outside and you'll have to come in soon."

"Let's play, Ana Isabel!"

Jaime's voice sounds like someone else's, it's stronger, louder. Has Jaime grown? How long had she been sick? Twenty days, says her mother.

"Do you want to hold my hand, Ana Isabel?"

The patio looks so different and seems so strange! Can it have gotten bigger? Smaller? The sun spreads up to the honeysuckle and reaches as high as the lattice. And the fountain, how smooth. "The big fish died, Ana Isabel!" The greediest one. Do you remember?"

The big fish died! And she also could have died and would not have been here now, next to Jaime, in the patio of her house...

There's Estefanía with her big kerchief tied around her head, the patchwork apron and her lips shaped like a hollowed out gourd.

Why should Estefania look so different? Isn't she the same old black woman? The one who walks her to school, who tells her ghost stories? Old Estefanía!

Why does everything look different, the patio, Jaime, and herself, as though she were another person?

"Be careful, Ana Isabel, there's a wasp!"

A wasp! There was a wasp on the sago palm. It's true there were always wasps flying around in the patio, on the begonia plants and the ripe guavas, but never on the sago palm. Those wasps sure work fast. They've made their home on top of the palm, a hard, enclosed house. The wasps go flying across the sun, beating their wings.

Jaime sat down in the shade of the chili pepper tree and builds up little piles of dirt that look like small hills. The sun momentarily hides behind the clouds. The patio cools down and becomes welcoming.

"Sit down, Ana Isabel. Weren't we gonna play?"

Ana Isabel sits down and pats the dirt with her hands. She takes a fistful of it and lets it slide through her fingers.

"Hey, Ana Isabel, here comes the sesame candy. It's almost twelve."

On the street, down below on the square, the shout grows louder.

"Alfodoque! Sesame sweets made by Elvira. With cheese and anise and sesame seeds!..."

Ana Isabel thinks about Elvira. Is she black like Estefanía and Domitila? Or white and freckled like Amelia? Her eyes might be squinty from moving the syrup pan close to the fire. Maybe she has little children around her asking to scrape the pan, just like she and Jaime do when their mother makes mango jelly.

"From Guare, sesame sweets!..."

Elvira is from Guare, where cider and brown sugar comes from.

"With cheese, anise and sesame!..."

The long, rhythmic call flies across the sunny square and suddenly grows louder.

"Ana Isabel, come, your lunch is ready!"

Her lunch! She almost forgot she was hungry. That it's going to be wonderful to be able to eat sitting up and dressed like before, it's been so long!

"Come, your soup is getting cold!"

Her mother brought her a big bowl of warm, steaming soup with a little sprig of mint, rounds of toast and a soft-boiled egg with its top cut off.

"What, how come Ana Isabel gets to eat eggs and I don't?"

"But child, can't you see she's sick?"

"Yes, she's sick alright. You always give her everything and nothing to me... Will you give me the top of the egg, Ana Isabel?"

The smell of mint wafts through the dining room. Ana Isabel breathes it in with her lips half-opened. She feels born again. As though she came back from a faraway remote country she did not want to go back to. How low the table is and how tall she is! The tablecloth is the same one, white and blue squares, but Ana Isabel repeatedly runs her hands over it as though she were touching it for the first time. And the cruet? Oil and vinegar, whose stopper Jaime will break one day and her mother will replace with a smaller one that will fit more snugly. The sugar bowl with the wide spoon Ana Isabel looks at her face with, her mouth on top and her eyes below.

"Eat, child, it will get cold!"

The bougainvillea has lost its leaves and only has flowers now. So red! Have they always been like that? Jaime brought his chair next to the table, facing Ana Isabel, to watch her eat.

"Give me the top, alright? Why aren't you eating, Ana Isabel? What are you thinking about?"

Could she even say what she's thinking about? About the sounds in the house. About Gregoria, who's blowing on the coals, about her mother who's pedaling on the sewing machine. About Estefanía's song, the recently poured cement, clean and shiny. About the whitewashed walls, the shutters banging in the wind. Could she even say what she's thinking about? About the noises in the street. About the footsteps of the people she doesn't know and diminish as they cross the corner. About the mangy dogs who run as they wag their tails, about surly cats that jump up on the tiles and meow pitifully. About the square. About the little Candelaria Square. About those who cross it, those whose names she doesn't know, about faces she's never seen... About the dust in the street, about the grass that grows between the stones, colored marbles. About little black Eusebio. Yes! Ana Isabel is thinking about little black Eusebio! Red flowers, the fragrant aroma of mint. The tablecloth, all the warm and cozy feeling of home fades away in the distance. Little black Eusebio suddenly appears above the familiar voices and gestures. Ana Isabel looks at him. She looks at his big sad eyes with their damp corneas, his wooly head, the white palms of his black hands. She hears his voice.

> *Where's the deer coming from!*
> *From the burning hill!*

"I didn't tell her, mommy. I didn't. It was her, only her... I didn't say it!"

Ana Isabel has fallen headfirst from the chair, her face drained of blood and her forehead broken out in a sweat. In the patio the wasps fly around the sago palm. The sun leaves yellow traces on the tablecloth. "I didn't tell her. It was her, only her..."

Mrs. Alcántara hurriedly comes and takes Ana Isabel in her arms. She cradles an immense, bottomless child's grief in her arms.

"It's nothing, my child, it's nothing. Have a sip of water. You're very weak. It was crazy for me to let you go out so soon..."

Ana Isabel opens her eyes. Everything looks white. A diffuse misty, pale white. A voice singing a song of the sea, with algae, with fish and sonorous sea shells. The whiteness spreads like steam. It engulfs the corners, it settles lightly over the sugar bowl, above the steaming bowl...

"Let's get you to your room, my child. Let's go..."

They walk slowly. The mother's arms, warm and gentle, wrapped around the little frail body.

Sitting next to the table, with his head in his hands, Jaime sobs.

The Lizard

"Ana Isabel, we're going to play Four Plants in the little square." Ana Isabel is combing her hair in front of the mirror near the console. She's wet her hair and is making curls with a piece of cane. She's spent half an hour in front of the mirror trying to change her silky, fine hair that falls straight over her shoulders into curls. A while ago they started playing the game in the square. It's the third time Jaime has come looking for her.

"But Ana Isabel, why are you combing your hair so much? You're not going to a party, as far as I know. Now you spend your time looking at yourself in the mirror and combing your hair."

Jaime is right. She's looking at herself in the mirror all the time. She curls her hair, she parts her hair first on one side, then in the middle, she sets waves with her mother's curlers, she wears ribbons...

"Come on, Ana Isabel, look, it's getting late!"

"Leave her alone, child. Why should she go with you? She's too old to go running around in the square with all those young boys. You're going to turn into a tomboy, Ana Isabel!"

But Jaime whispers softly so Mrs. Alcántara won't hear, "Don't be silly, come on. You know who's playing with us? Pepe, come on, you blockhead!" Pepe doesn't wear bangs now. He wears his hair combed back like a grown up young man and he doesn't tell Ana Isabel she's ugly. While he is playing with her he comes closer.

"Your hair looks nice, Ana Isabel!"

Ana Isabel had blushed to the very roots of her golden hair. Pepe stood there looking at her and then ran his hands across her hair. That afternoon, the sun wasn't shining. The tops of the trees were hidden in shadow. The bells stopped ringing and the last peals were lost in the alleyway behind the church.

"But what are you doing there, standing around like idiots? One, two, three, you're it, Ana Isabel!"

Folks on the street don't call her ugly, either. She's grown and her skin is smooth and tight. When she goes to school Estefanía doesn't let her go running alone like she used to.

"Stay close to me, child, don't run ahead..."

She spends her time looking at herself in the mirror.

"All right, I'm going. I'm not going to wait for you any longer. You never want to play anymore."

She never wants to play! When she goes out to the square she stands there looking at the trees and the church tower. What's happening to Ana Isabel? Why does she suddenly feel like crying for no reason? Isn't she happy? Hasn't she bought patent-leather shoes like Cecilia's? Why does she feel so alone? All the children in the square are always asking her to play. There's a father who loves her, her brother Jaime who even gave her a box of candy for her birthday. There's her mother who kisses her, who leans over to pat her gently at night... What's happening to Ana Isabel? Everything makes her sigh. When the buds in the rose bush bloom. If the magnolia has new buds... A butterfly, a dead ant, make her shiver.

"But Ana Isabel, why are you standing there with your mouth open? What are you thinking about?"

Jaime slammed the door on his way out. Ana Isabel continues to curl her hair around the piece of cane. The curls refuse to form. She'll wear the red ribbon. She'll gather her hair on her neck and leave the ends loose, floating over her shoulders. Shouts and laughter are coming from the square. The afternoon is clear and blue. It rained this morning, the grass soaked it up and it looks like it's grown. The sky is washed clean. Fine delicate clouds cap the sky.

"But are you still planted there in front of the mirror? Your hair is going to fall out from you combing it so much, child! Leave your hair alone, Ana Isabel!"

Now they're not playing Four Plants any more. Ana Isabel, standing by the door looks at the smaller square with the flowers. They're not there, either. Domitila is walking by in the middle of the street.

"Hello, girl. My how you've grown! You're going to be a young lady..."

Ana Isabel is wearing her pink dress. The sleeves are too short and they show off her tan arms. She crosses the street and walks into the square. The bells haven't rung to call to prayer yet. Through the slender branches of the kapok tree she can see the sky lighting up in the dusk.

"Come on, Ana Isabel, we're gonna burn a lizard!"

Jaime can hardly speak. He's come running. The excited words fill his mouth.

"Come, come..."

Ana Isabel walks quickly, dragged by Jaime.

Crouching in the dirt, they are burning the lizard. Pepe is directing the procedure. He has a box of matches in his hand. They've dug a deep hole to put the lizard in. Then they covered it with dry leaves and are about to light the fire. They all speak in hushed tones. Their eyes are shining and their faces are flushed. Pepe's hair falls forward and covers his eyes. He hasn't turned around to look at Ana Isabel.

"It's not moving..."

"It must be dead..."

The burning leaves twist and crackle.

There is a smell of burned resin. The thick dark smoke burns their eyes.

"Squat down here, Ana Isabel, so you can see."

Ana Isabel doesn't want to get her pink dress dirty. Besides, she's afraid to come closer. A lizard!

"And why are you killing it?"

"You always come out with such nonsense. Why? Because we feel like it!"

Pepe stands up and shakes away the dirt that had stuck to his knees. He throws his hair back violently.

"What's the matter, Ana Isabel? Are you going to start crying?"

"But it's a lizard. Isn't it a living thing?"

"Leave her alone, man, that's how women are…"

He's still holding the box of matches in his hand. He lights one slowly, then another… The little flames hardly light up when they are quickly blown out by the breeze.

"Matches," says Pepe, shaking the box in his hand, "who's got matches?"

He's up on his feet, taller than the rest, looking at Ana Isabel over his shoulder. He puts the box away in his pocket, turns abruptly around and walks away whistling. "Whoever wants to can follow me," he exclaims before walking away. Everyone walks behind Pepe who is already crossing the corner with long strides. Ana Isabel is left alone. Now there's hardly any smoke. Only a small sound the fire makes as it dies out among the leaves. Ana Isabel lies down on the ground. She's not worried about getting her pink dress dirty. There's the lizard. Still hot. Twisted like a curled leaf, like the bark of a tree, like the velvet scraps her mother keeps in a bag that Ana Isabel loves to take out and look at. It no longer has the lovely colors it had when it ran over stones. Yellow, bright green… Its eyes are empty. Ana Isabel holds it close to her heart. She touches its shrunken stomach with the tips of her fingers. Surely it has guts and even a heart that beats like all the world's living creatures… The afternoon silence engulfs the square. Down below the trolley runs past with its lights on.

The Lizard

A girl pushes a hoop around with her hands around the statue. The bell tolls harshly and sorrowfully. The bells are ringing because it's November. November is the month of the dead. The bells are ringing for all who have died. Who are dead to the sky and the cold moon. To the stars that scatter and go around and die...of colorless flowers. The death of earth and dust, of dry leaves. Of smoke that dies away slowly. The death of the square in the shadows... The bells toll for the dead...

Ana Isabel
on the Other Side of the Bars

I t's nighttime. Everyone in the Alcántara household is asleep. Everyone? No. Ana Isabel is awake. She wants to turn on the light but she's afraid to make noise and then her mother will come.

"What's going on Ana Isabel? You're always afraid. Sleep soundly, child!"

She'll have to turn on the light. She has to reassure herself she's not having a nightmare from which she'll wake up laughing and sighing. Why is she squeezing her hands until it hurts? Why doesn't she fall asleep calmly while she tells herself stories about brave heroines, about ballerinas in airy tulle dresses who dance with their lovely round arms raised up high? Is she perhaps afraid of the dead? Now she's not afraid of the Cart of the Souls or of the Mula Manía. The Cart of the Souls used to make her cover her ears whenever a cart passed by in the early morning, carrying the evil eye with its yellow light and a lurching driver with sleepy songs on his lips... The Mula Manía, that made her tremble every time an old mule passed by trudging and striking the cobblestones with its hooves... When she was younger Ana Isabel was so frightened by the stories that Ermengilda, Alcántara's freed housemaid told her about burials, ghosts, spirits and a horse galloping in the night. A phantom horse that crossed the patio and disappeared into the corridor... Now Ana Isabel is older, but she's still afraid of the dead. Of the dead who mysteriously disappear into the night and you never see again. Of the dead who can come back in this restless hour when night is also dying, they can come back and take her by the hand and squeeze her tightly with their cold bones... But it's not the dead who're making Ana Isabel tremble tonight... She'll have to turn out the light to make sure it's true. Is she going to die? Is she going to bleed to death little by little until there is no blood left? Until she's white, as white as the lilies the mule drivers bring down from the hills on their backs. White as chalk, as lime, cold and white like death itself... Could death be silently approaching? But it's not her death. It's the same thing that happened to Justina and Cecilia. And Justina is alive, very much alive, with her blue eyes and her plump freckled hands.

"You are a woman now," her mother told her. "Now you have to be careful."

Justina's not dead. Her legs are shapely and you can see her breasts under her high school blouse. And Cecilia? Cecilia was taken out of school because according to her mother, she was too old to be crossing so many streets. The same thing had happened to everyone and one day Esperanza Caldera stained her piqué dress. That morning math class was interrupted. The teacher took Esperanza Caldera, who was pale and frightened, by the hand and everyone was afraid, whispering in low voices. The same thing had happened to all of them. Ana Isabel didn't ignore the fact that the same thing would happen to her one day. But, my Lord, why does it have to be today? She'll have to tell her mother. And what if her father finds out? And her little brother Jaime? The cement is cool and her bare feet are burning. The parlor windows are closed. She'll have to open them softly, without making a sound so she can look out at the square. How lovely the square looks. The little Candelaria Square! It doesn't look the same. There's the tree, the big fig trees, the empty benches... There's the smaller square with its zinnias and its red and yellow crotons. From the window you can barely see the smaller square with flowers where Ana Isabel chased butterflies with a net attached to a pole. Lower down is

Otilia's house but Otilia doesn't live there. Her father took off one day and Otilia's mother waited for him for many months but he never came back. Where could Otilia's father have gone off to this time? Perhaps to the plains, where there are no hills to look at, where there is nothing but savannah, savannah, and more savannah. Ana Isabel hasn't been to the plains, but Gregoria told her about it, because Gregoria is from Zaraza and there are many nights when she is shivering with fever... Maybe he went to the plains and died one afternoon when the savannah was all golden and the guacarachas were sleeping with their heads under their wings. Otilia's mother took a job working as a maid and Otilia ran away with her cousin one night. Ana Isabel came across her on the street wearing high heels and lipstick. Some old maids who make candy now live in Otilia's house and Consuelo the islander sells it. Consuelo always comes by at noon with her starched skirts, her big colorful checkered kerchief, a small straw hat and a very white round pad high on her head holding up the tray. You would think the old spinsters were fairies, that's how fine and delicate their sweets are. They make candied coconut sweets, soursop desserts, boxes of eggs, and little white toasted almidones. Ana Isabel has been there to buy sweets and to visit the house where Otilia used to live. From the entryway you can smell the guavas cooking and the fresh scent of caramel. The evening primroses are in bloom and the ferns hanging from the beams spill over their manes of hair. Ana Isabel hangs back in the entryway waiting for the sweets remembering how she waited for Otilia to exchange trading cards or to go skating. The older of the spinsters is thin and hunchbacked and her speech is as slow as molasses. The house has a small square patio where Otilia's mother used to spread the coffee beans out to dry before roasting them. That's because Otilia's mother used to sell coffee in yellow paper bags. Ana Isabel had helped to move the wooden paddle over the steaming kettle many times and she left with her eyes red and her throat burning. The antechamber and gallery, both of them small, face the patio and it's as though Otilia with her dark eyes and brown face is about to come out. The old spinsters bring the sweets wrapped up in fluffy white paper. Ana Isabel buys a potato-shaped sweet with a clove on top and little boxes of sugared eggs in their paper cups. Because the sweets the old spinsters make are fine and delicate. Not like the home-made sweets Pepe's mother makes that she sells in the afternoons in the square. Rosario no longer makes home-made sweets because Pepe is now a clerk in Los Desaparados, a new grocery store that just opened, with labeled gold bottles all lined up, jars of preserves and big sacks full of grain leaning against the doors. Ana Isabel walks by slowly when she passes by but Estefanía won't let her go in like she'd like to.

"Why go in there, girl? To hear ugly things and look at dizzy drunken men?"

Ana Isabel slows down her pace and picks up a handful of beans while Pepe makes a face and winks at her. The street below can't be seen from the window because it's still night and there's still no light. That's where Perico and Carmencita used to go to play cops and robbers in the square. Ana Isabel used to wait for them lying down on the grass full of burrs, chasing swiftly leaping stick-bugs. Perico is all grown up now and he helps out in his father's business. He spends his days loading sacks of coal and knocking on doors with his stained hands. He attends night school. He knows how to read and he studies his times tables. Ana Isabel grabs hold of the bars in her shaking hands. They are cold and damp from the night, the cold December night. It must be very late because a diffuse light, a blue-white light descends on the tops of the trees. The church tower stands out in its stillness. The bells are

105

silent. Soon they will let their clearest song fly. It's December, the month of Christmas, of hymns sung by thin children's voices. Soon the church doors will open and one will hear the first peals calling out to Mass. Old ladies chilled by the fog wrapped up in thick black dirty shawls will cross the square and boys will skate on the lower street where they've just poured macadam. The sound of the skates will reach up to the window where Ana Isabel is standing, like the sound of the distant flow of an unending river. They haven't poured macadam on Ana Isabel's street yet, or on the little street that's behind the church. The stones are still there where Ana Isabel lay down to listen to Francisco's hammering. But Francisco isn't there anymore. He died one rainy morning and the stones were half submerged under the yellow water and clumps of earth. He died from an intestinal infection that would not get better, despite the sage and borage Estefanía picked for him from the ravine. He didn't have a wife or children, did Francisco, or brothers or sisters, either. No one knew if he had any relatives, but they carried him to the cemetery on their shoulders. The entryway stood open just like when Francisco hammered away with his mouth full of nails. It was raining and people took shelter in the small parlor where Francisco was laid out. There was Domitila and Amelia and Concha, the one who makes corn cachapas and Eladio's aunt, the one who never leaves the house, with her hard face pocked from smallpox. Ruperto the coal man brought Perico and Carmencita. Carmencita, dressed in black, sat in a corner on a broken stool. Pepe brought rum from the store and the men started swearing and spitting through their teeth. The women talked about plasters and herbs and about Francisco who hadn't gotten better maybe of some evil wish they'd sent him? Francisco's body didn't weigh much on the shoulders of the men who carried him. His obscure and humble life of a shoe repair man weighed so little! They slowly made their way through the street, dragging their feet like in a procession... Ana Isabel had followed them with her eyes as they turned the corner. The bells are calling to Christmas Mass. Ana Isabel continues to look at the square from her window. How she wants to leave, to run away, to flee from the Alcántara house and lose herself across the square! To slip through the window like she did when she was small and she was playing hide-and-seek. How she loved to hide! Always fearful and anxious her hands cold and her heart beating fast in her chest. She would hide in the corner of the armoire, behind the flowered curtain. She crouched in the dark corner next to her father's jacket and her grandfather's silk cap. The curtain stuck to her face and released the smell of stale old dust. She hid in the armoire with the mirror. Her mother helped her to climb in and would slowly close the creaking doors. It happened at night, in the armoire and Ana Isabel heard only the beating of her heart. She stood there without moving being careful not to trip over the cardboard boxes on the bottom of the armoire and the tin box of Maria biscuits that had a country girl with a white apron and round red cheeks in which her mother kept her needles and thread... Ana Isabel curled up next to her mother's clothes next to the black dress her mother wore in times of mourning, or she wore for many days when one of her father's uncles whom Ana Isabel never met died. There was the gray dress and the one with the seed pattern which looked so good on her mother, she looked so young and gay in that bright dress. Ana Isabel knew her mother's dresses by heart. Old dresses that had been re-sewn thousands of times. Made over each year, now with a collar, now with a ribbon, or by shortening the sleeves. Dresses turned inside out with the seams ripped apart and an added piece of new cloth so they would look different... Her mother's old dresses that held her scent and her shape, and were a little bit of her, right there hanging and still. Ana Isabel inhaled her mother's scent. The smell of her hands, of her delicate fingers, of her gray hair, of her tender smile... Her mother's scent interwoven with lullabies and tender words. Her mother's old scent that had been close to her before, since forever, from even before she knew her name was Ana Isabel! From inside the armoire muted voices reached as if from afar and Ana Isabel trembled when she heard Jaime's footsteps, when he opened the door shouting," What a blockhead! I knew all along you were hiding in the armoire! You always hide in the same place, Ana Isabel!" But her greatest pleasure was to hide in the parlor window. She sat in the window sill with her feet between the bars while her mother closed the shutters from the inside, while her feet hung out onto the street. She scraped the wall with her feet and the floor beneath filled with white flakes like bread crumbs. That would be in the afternoon when the square was always deserted. Ana Isabel spent a long time scraping the wall with her legs hanging out and then she would slip through the bars and head to the square running. There she found Jaime hiding in the ficus pulling thorns. "That's not fair, Ana Isabel, to come through the square. That's cheating!" The bells continued to chime, pealing gaily announcing Christmas Mass. A rosy light, like water descended from the hills. Now the branches of the trees can be seen. Ana Isabel is always standing up looking at the square. She could run away like when she played hide-and-seek. Slip through the bars and leave her home, the Alcántara house, squeezing between the bars, running free, filled with the morning's cold! She could run away like when she was small and reach the ravine, climb to the savannah and get lost in the tall grass, among the yellow flowers... She could slip away like when she was young... But her shoulders are too wide and they keep her from getting out between the bars. Like Justina, she has tiny little breasts that you can see under the fine cloth. Her legs aren't thin and a slight and lovely curve insinuated itself on her hips. Her body, her woman's body confined, held back by the bars! Her body must remain still, a prisoner in the Alcántara house! Now she can't run through the square, or go climb up on the roof, or climb up into the branches of the mango tree! Her legs won't skip over the mossy stones in the ravine. In the savannah, her kite with stars and moons and its defiant tail won't sing her younger song, cruising through the sky, breaking its wings against the clouds. Now she won't look at birds and flowers with the clear eyes of a child. When she walks across the patio where the ants are marching all in a row, hurrying and working hard, Ana Isabel will perhaps be thinking about the sorrow of life. The sorrow of love, and without meaning to she'll step on the ants... The world of her childhood, with its rivers, hills, clouds, clouds that looked like ships! Sinbad the Sailor's white ships! The world of her childhood will stay here, under the tree, under the big fig trees, in the cool shade of the ficus next to the broken benches... The sun is warming things up. The birds are flying down from high up on the treetops and they are circling on the grass. The square is visible between the bars. Ana Isabel is on the other side of the bars...

Other little children who aren't Perico, or Carmencita or Eladio, or Pepe the altar boy or little black Eusebio. Little Black Eusebio for whom Ana Isabel dreamed up a coat of arms, a very pretty one with a colt with its tail raised up high. Other little children are playing in the square.

"Bogey Man, Bogey Man will rip your eyes out!"

Little children wearing ragged clothes, broken alpargatas. Perhaps some respectable girls like Ana Isabel will play, clasping her little hands with them. They'll play Doñana or Rice Pudding.

Ana Isabel: A Respectable Girl

Rice pudding, Rice pudding, I want to marry
A little widow from the capital...

Ana Isabel can't see them. She's standing up with her eyes wide open, next to the window, but she can't see them. A veil of rain, a thin rain of tears envelops them and makes them seem far away. The voices come from afar, wet from the invisible rain. Thrushes and yellow orioles peck at insects between the blades of dry grass. From the tops of the kapok tree small white tufts, like snowflakes, snowflakes of memory and nostalgia drift down. Through the fine rain of tears, behind the bars, Ana Isabel watches them fall...

THE END

Glossary

Alfondoque: a kind of candy made with dark sugar, cheese, anise and sesame seeds.

Alpargatas: rope soled espadrilles worn in rural areas of Venezuela.

Arepa: a flatbread made of maize dough, or corn cake, eaten daily in Venezuela.

Bolívar: a coin.

Burriquita: "Little Donkey," the female donkey, a folkloric dance.

Cachapa: corn-based pancake.

Calleja: Saturnino Calleja Ferná (1853-1915) was a Spanish autor and an editor of children's books.

Casabe: Cassava bread.

Carato: a sweet corn drink.

Chucuto: the dog's name implies that he is short and squat or crippled.

Corridos: folk songs.

Doñana or *Doña Ana*: a traditional children's circle game in which one child stands in the middle while the others sing: "Doña Ana está en su jardín" or "Doña Ana is in her garden."

Galerones: songs from the Venezuelan plains.

Guarapo: a fermented drink made with brown sugar.

Guacharaca: Penelope bird, cocrico.

Guasimo: a tree common to the plains of Venezuela which produces and acid-tasting fruit.

Hallaca: traditional Christmas dish, much like Mexican tamales, but the various ingredients are wrapped in banana leaves.

Joropo: a folk dance from the "llanos" or the plains.

La Mula Manía or *La Mata Carmelera*: a legend which may have African origins about a bad woman who is converted into a spirit, a phantasm or specter.

La Negra: the appellation "The Black" followed by a black woman's first name is a common and not derogatory way to refer to women of African descent. Venezuela abolished slavery in 1816.

Lieds: Romantic German art songs composed for voice and piano.

Locha: a coin used between 1896-1969, equivalent to about 12 cents.

Majarete: Corn pudding.

Malojillo: lemon grass.

Maracaibo: a lake in northwest Venezuela. The original inhabitants of this region were Arawaks and Caribs. Legend has it that when the native chief named Mara fell when he resisted the Spanish during a battle, the Indians shouted "Mara cayó" or Mara fell.

Papelón: a bar of unrefined cane sugar.

Primus: a pressurized- burner or kerosene stove.

Pan de bolívar: a bun that costs one bolívar.

Pan de horno: a sweet empanada filled with papaya or bananas.

Poco a poco Míster Payer: an onomatopoeic chant that mimics the sound of the train chugging along.

Reales: a denomination of money.

Salgari: Emilio Salgari (1862-1911), Italian writer of more than two hundred adventure stories. He is considered a pioneer of science fiction.

Afterword: A Few Words from a Reader

RoseAnna Mueller asked Miguel Frontado, a Venezuelan who helped her with the translation and had never read the book, to share his thoughts after reading it. Here is his moving description:

Reading Antonia Palacios is going back in time to my childhood and school days. Caracas born and raised, I had the chance to know all the places she describes in *Ana Isabel, una niña decente*. The most remarkable retrospective journey I got from the story is about the Candelaria Square, a huge place I used to go to play in with my cousins in my childhood. But Palacios describes a Caracas from a time I did not know. She describes what Venezuelans know as *Caracas vieja* (old Caracas), a little town connected by dirt roads to other settlements nearby. Nowadays all those places in the book are part of the huge metropolis Caracas became in the late 70s. The book takes me to my memories about the beach. It takes me to my school days, when I would dream about going all over the Venezuelan coast to get to know all the beautiful beaches the country has. It makes me recall those times when Caracas was a place for everyone. The city grew, but the places in the book still live as though time has not gone by. To read the book is to travel in time and space, taking out the modern façades and setting up the old mud walls in the individually named corners of Caracas. It brings me to that, to the particular naming of the streets, to the ice-cream man on the corner, to the smell of sweet *arepas*, to the old videos about *generalissimo* Juan Vicente Gómez's dictatorship, to the history books, to the old yellow Venezuelan maps posted on the walls, to what I enjoyed in my early youth.

It is also an enlightened journey to the background of Venezuelan society. A society where everybody has a place, with a diversity that makes us rich. What brings me satisfaction is knowing that the good Venezuelan of the 1900s is still there, with a pocket full of hope, looking forward to better times to come. The hope of the working man who rises early and works hard every day, smiling in the morning after a nice, hot cup of coffee.

113

Universitas Press
Books that make sense of the world

Also from Universitas Press:

www.universitaspress.com
facebook.com/universitaspress
@UniversitasP

Printed in the USA
CPSIA information can be obtained
at www.ICGtesting.com
LVHW050551241124
797436LV00002B/182